TEXAS WARRIOR

TEXAS WARRIOR

James Kane

GUNSMOKE

First published in the UK by Hale

This hardback edition 2011
by AudioGO Ltd
by arrangement with
Golden West Literary Agency

ISBN 978 1 408 46315 4

British Library Cataloguing in Publication Data available.

Printed and bound in Great Britain by
CPI Antony Rowe, Chippenham and Eastbourne

Peter B. Germano was born the oldest of six children in New Bedford, Massachusetts. During the Great Depression, he had to go to work before completing high school. It left him with a powerful drive to continue his formal education later in life, finally earning a Master's degree from Loyola University in Los Angeles in 1970. He sold his first Western story to A.A. Wyn's Ace Publishing magazine group when he was twenty years old. In the same issue of *Sure-Fire Western* (1/39) Germano had two stories, one by Peter Germano and the other by Barry Cord. He came to prefer the Barry Cord name for his Western fiction. When the Second World War came, he joined the U.S. Marine Corps. Following the war he would be called back to active duty, again as a combat correspondent, during the Korean conflict. In 1948 Germano began publishing a series of Western novels, either as Barry Cord or **James/Jim Kane**, stories notable for their complex plots while the scenes themselves are simply set, with a minimum of description and quick character sketches employed to establish a wide assortment of very different personalities. The pacing, which often seems swift due to the adept use of a parallel plot structure (narrating a story from several different viewpoints), is combined in these novels with atmospheric descriptions of weather and terrain. *Dry Range* (1955), *The Sagebrush Kid* (1954), *The Iron Trail Killers* (1960), and *Trouble in Peaceful Valley* (1968) are among his best Westerns. "The great southwest . . ." Germano wrote in 1982, "this is the country, and these are the people that gripped my imagination . . . and this is what I have been writing about for forty years. And until I die I shall remain the little New England boy who fell in love with the 'West,' and as a man had the opportunity to see it and live in it."

TEXAS WARRIOR

I

Chuck Powers jogged his bay horse along Broken Bow's principal thoroughfare on a late summer night with a full red moon riding low behind him. He asked the first man he met the location of the livery stable. Chuck was considerate of the animal that had carried him well over a thousand miles in his long pursuit of a man.

From the Texas-Mexican border to the Wyoming sheep country was more than two thousand miles of desert and mountains, of lush-grassed valley and treeless plains. He had put up in quiet towns and bad ones; he had ridden through land parched by drought and soggy with rain; he had suffered through winter snows and blazing summer heat.

And in the process Chuck Powers, lean and quiet-faced and trailing a man he wanted badly to find, had been remolded.

There was little of the happy carelessness that had marked him a year ago; none in his voice. At the moment he was tired and depressed, yielding to the conviction that his quarry had definitely escaped him.

"There's an extra cartwheel for you if my horse is tended to right," he told a somewhat curious stableman. "I'm too tired to do more than find a place where I can drop asleep. I'll take any suggestion you have."

"Down the street." The stableman pointed. "Down where a bunch of horses is tied to the rail. Not the first—the second place. That's the Cactus Bar. Best likker, best food, an' upstairs, as clean a sleeping place as can be found in the county."

He cast a glance down to Powers' gunbelt, remembered the double cinch around the belly of the bay behind them and guessed:

"Texan? New Mexico?"

"First is right," Powers said. "Well, reckon I'll check in at the Cactus Bar."

"You staying in town?"

Chuck shook his head. "Be leaving in the morning," he told the stableman. "Heading north. . . ."

He didn't have to tell the stable hand that, but he was doing his thinking aloud. He had been in too many towns this past year, always asking the same question;

he was tired of it now.

Maybe I'll feel better in the morning, he thought as he made his way slowly down the street toward the combination saloon-hotel the stableman had recommended. And as always, he was conscious of the slight rub of his holsters, the weight and the feel and the meaning of the heavy .35's at his belt. They were symbols of the task he had set for himself—what he had sworn to accomplish, and seemingly now had failed to achieve.

He saw the horses now, bunched up at the rail in front of the saloon, and by habit his glance studied each brand. He did not see the horse or the brand he wanted, but he was too tired to be disappointed.

All he wanted was a place to sleep. In the morning he'd ask a few questions, pick up his horse and ride on.

He pushed the batwings open and started toward the bar. He was aware of others in the room, but he had his eye on the beefy, thick-mustached man behind the counter in front of him. Chuck did not look around. He crossed to the bar and waited a moment for the bartender to notice him. But the man behind the bar was paying no attention to newcomers. Nor, it appeared, was anyone else.

A harsh voice, not directed at him, pulled Powers

around. He gazed with growing interest at the scene which was holding the bartender's rapt attention. And a scowl formed on his brow at the unfairness of what he saw.

Four to one were not betting odds—not when a man's life depended on it!

Four men armed with ugly-looking shotguns surrounded a lone man seated at a card table close to the outside wall. They made a silent tableau at the moment— a dramatic picture of angry faces and postures. Even the audience scattered among the tables in the rear of the room sat rigid; the bartender, resting his weight on the cherrywood counter, stood stiffly. It was a scene frozen in time, weighted with the expectancy of the harsh question Powers had heard—a question remaining unanswered.

Then the answer came, and for Powers the strangeness and the timelessness of the scene passed. He was in a familiar world once more, witness to a quarrel among men.

"I'm telling you flat out," the man at the table was saying coldly, "I wasn't there! An' none of my boys did it. We ain't got the time to waste on you poor mutton nurses!"

That was nerve, Powers thought.

The shotgun muzzles were not four feet away from the

speaker, and the business end of a sawed-off 20-gauge generally created disturbing effects. Powers heard a slight murmur of admiration run through the room. A quite different emotion seeped through Chuck's weary brain. Sheepmen! Only a Texas cattle hand could understand the contempt which went with the word. The buckaroos farther north did not know it—and the man at bay at the table talked Texas, not Wyoming.

Slowly Powers moved closer to the scene, his duty in the matter too plain for a Texan to shirk.

The men with the shotguns were angry. There was not the least shade of doubt regarding that point. One, a burly, tattered giant, fairly quivered in the grip of his rage. His face was distorted with it—congested, wild.

"Damn you, Turner, you're lyin' through your teeth! More, you're a dirty, murderin' liar!"

Powers tensed automatically. Back where he came from, a man killed anyone who called him that.

But the crisis passed. Evidently Turner, the man at the table, had brains as well as courage. It was plain and useless suicide to make a move. The sheepmen meant business.

"You'll pay for that, Burton," Turner answered. He was smiling as he said it, but his smile was forced. "If you and yore friends were anywhere near white, you'd give me the even break I'm entitled to!"

"You've got it!" stated Powers dispassionately.

He was standing not ten feet behind the group now, his drawn Colts gleaming dully in the lamplight. "I'm takin' cards in this game, boys." He aimed the words at the sheepmen. "All moves will be slow and careful. *Careful!*" he snapped, and the authority in his voice stopped the man called Burton, whose impulse was plainly geared to pivoting for a quick desperate shot at him.

"Careful, everybody!" Powers was Texas-drawling his words now, the tension in his shoulders ebbing. "I don't know who's who an' what's what here. But four to one ain't a square shot to give *any* man. Second, I'm a cowman, or was, an' I ain't standin' by while a cowman tangles with mutton wranglers." He paused briefly, then went on, his voice sharpening. "The speech being over, the party moves. You, Turner, first—get up and stand with yore back to the wall—"

Turner had half risen, his right hand crooked just above his gunbutt. His regular, somewhat dark features showed the release of his clamped emotions. The whole affair, Powers saw, hung on the balance of very small things—some sudden starts—some surge of courage, or rage, or the impulse of whatever reason had brought the sheepmen there to face Turner in the first place.

Powers judged all the factors, his gray eyes cold and watchful. The shotguns could be swung sharply around; his position was none too secure. He had a dead drop on them, and what he could do with Colts was not included in the ordinary abilities of most men. But shotguns sprayed—just enough at that distance.

He tensed again as the sheepman, Burton, began to move.

Interruption eased the painful balance of life and death. Powers heard horses stop outside, a noise at the saloon door. He saw Burton and his companions exchange glances, lose their wild indecision. The three smaller sheepmen showed fear now.

A girl and four cowboys entered. Powers did not move, trusting his instincts which sounded no warning. But the girl's voice, incisive and confident in spite of its softness, surprised him. Gunplay was a man's business.

"Joe, what is the matter? They haven't hurt you, have they?"

She passed into Chuck's field of vision, and he realized that a homespun skirt and plain blouse could look marvelously unlike anything they had ever resembled before. A new feeling came over him at once, and remained. But it did not affect either thought or action. Easily he sheathed his Colts and moved backward toward the bar.

"Reckon sentry duty's yourn now, boys," he said calmly to the group who had entered with the girl. Not until he spoke the words did he turn around to appraise them, receiving a return scrutiny that was both approving and curious.

"We'll take it, stranger," one answered, balancing a weapon in his right hand. "Fact is, we got it—took it the minnit we came in. An' them polecats know it."

Powers grinned through a returning weariness.

"I feel closer to home than I've been in seven months," he remarked to the man, while watching Turner and the girl.

"What part of Texas *you* from?" he added, smiling with a sense of kinship.

"Well, I swum in the Brazos when I was a boy," began the other. Then, abruptly: "What's that, Joe? Oh, take them outside!"

Joe was Turner's name. Powers' lids drooped wearily as the four sheepmen were marched out of the saloon at the point of Colt muzzles. The interest he felt was swiftly waning—only the girl in homespun arrested his yawn, and the desire to ask the bartender for sleeping accommodations.

She was coming over to him.

"We want to thank you, Mr.—"

"Powers," supplied the tall, dusty figure before her with a tired grin. "Chuck Powers, ma'am—a shrinking violet—traveler looking for a place to lay his tired head."

He saw her dark eyes grow darker in puzzled surprise for just a moment, then laugh up at him merrily.

"You didn't look like the shrinking type at all at the moment we entered. Joe and I wish to thank you, Mr. Powers. They might have killed him because he was helpless. Otherwise—"

Powers' intuition put in the missing words. Evidently this girl loved Joe Turner and was proud of her man.

"He no doubt would have messed them up some," he said lightly. "Four to one doesn't mean anything to a Texan."

"You are from Texas yourself, Mr. Powers?"

"Yeah—sort of on the edges. What you planning to do with them sheepherders?" he shifted, addressing Turner, who had come to join them.

"Put them in jail for now, until the law gets ready to move. Crazy as loons they were—accusing *me* of driving their sheep herds over rock fall and killing two herders." The man was indignant. "Taking me for a measly skunk like that! You'll pardon my talking like this, Sandra— but I'm all flustered over it. I've been trying my best not to fight—'cause we're marrying soon," he explained to Powers, "and a marrying man's got to gentle down. But—"

"Somebody keeps prodding you, eh?" Powers grinned. Mentally he gave Turner credit for other things besides nerve. The man was an impressive talker, and he was remarkably good-looking.

"Never mind, Joe," Sandra told him, her voice conveying things which reminded Powers of a certain well known adage.

"Well, I reckon the ruckus's over," he said. "And I'm sleepy besides. Glad I met you, Turner—and you, Miss Sandra."

He touched his hat to her as he went out.

II

Chuck Powers slept well, the deep, dreamless sleep induced by extreme fatigue. A morning sun, warming his face, gradually roused his senses. With a grateful stretching of refreshed muscles, he rolled out of bed, dressed, and went downstairs, where the amount of bacon and eggs he consumed brought questioning and admiring remarks from the Cactus Bar morning cook.

After the meal, he sauntered out and walked uptown, smoking a cigaret. He turned in at the town stables where he had left his horse the night before.

"Broken Bow," he remarked to no one in particular, "you're a cussed nice town. You ain't noisy, like some I been through—and you ain't dusty—much. Only one fault you got—your citizens act like they never saw guns before. Which is a state of affairs which just can't be."

He mentioned this fact to the stableman before mounting his rested horse.

"Don't dodge it, *compadre*," he pressed the man. "You

made goggle eyes yourself last night, and even now. Ain't you ever seen two guns worn before?"

"Sure, sure," the other replied, fingering a bright new silver dollar Chuck gave him. The extra coin helped him attain a confidential attitude. "It ain't that, stranger. Broken Bow's been peaceful an' law-abiding a long time, but most of the cattlemen and their hands still wear shooting irons. Habit, mostly. It's what you done last night—you an' Joe Turner ain't the usual thing around here, see? Gunmen from Texas don't come to Broken Bow every day."

"No, reckon they don't," Powers said idly. He swung up into the saddle. From his higher altitude, he surveyed the man on the ground.

"So Joe Turner's a gunman, eh?"

"Ah—well—yeah. He's caused trouble around here, anyway. Cleaned out one rustlers' nest in the hills; bears down hard on all valley sheepherders. Texas style, he claims. Some of the ranchers are glad he's come—some, like Tommy Boyd of the Box Circle brand, ain't. An' of course, *I* got no interest—"

" 'Course not," Powers agreed diplomatically. "Joe Turner just get here?"

"Two months ago. He's now foreman of the SV spread up north a ways. Gonna marry the girl who owns it—you seen her last night. Sandra Vaughn. Her old man was real white. He died a while back, and she quit teaching school here in Broken Bow to go up an' run the ranch. Turner came along; trouble came up; he settled it an' a future for himself. Pretty soft, I say—"

"Yeah," Powers drawled, interrupting. "Well, *compadre*—I'm saluting you and Broken Bow." About to touch reins to his horse's neck, he turned again, and his features went hard at the mood brought on by his own questions—questions he had asked scores of times in dozens of different places.

"You didn't happen to see a rider on a big black hoss come through here, did yuh? Anywhere inside of three weeks time, say? You should remember them if you saw them. The hoss was big, bigger'n most—all black with a white stocking on a front leg—I ain't sure which one. An' he had funny ears, that hoss. Bullet cut through the nerves. They hung dead, making him easy to pick out of any cavvy. You recollect seeing a hoss like that?"

The stableman felt slightly chilled.

"No," he answered in the presence of something beyond his understanding, his gaze on Chuck's rock-hard face. "I ain't seen no such hoss, mister."

Powers came back to normal.

"Well, *adios.*" He waved, and set his horse to canter

up the street.

The stableman gazed thoughtfully after him.

Powers rode west toward the hills, through gray and monotonous sagebrush. Ahead of him, apparently nearby, the buckles of ground were treeless except for the presence of green splotches that marked spots where quaking aspen and cottonwood fringed some hidden creek. The sun lost its mellowness, beat down with white-hot vigor. Noon found him at the first climb.

He rested in a cleft among rocks, grateful for the shade and the luck which brought a flock of sage hens by. The unexpected addition to his beans extended the noon stop by a half-hour, and when he rode off again, up into the hills, a full stomach brought musings and impulses he had choked for months.

Of a sudden he felt lonely, starkly lonely, out in the big emptiness of plain and hills, without chuck wagon talk to look forward to at evening time. He had been apart from all range contacts for months, following a phantom trail—a trail of a black stallion with flop ears. And the trail had faded. For weeks now no one he had asked had seen the lop-eared black horse. The trail had been fairly decipherable through all of Texas and the corners of four other states. It had faded in the Yellowtail country—left him with only a sense of angry futility.

Riding along again, he thought of Sandra Vaughn, a girl he had seen once, and of a man named Turner. They, he reflected, had things to live for.

"Hello!" he muttered in surprise, his faculties suddenly leaving useless thoughts to concentrate on very material objects ahead.

He was riding in a shallow coulee, a long, winding gulch between rounded rises. A horseman had appeared at top of the left rise, and was paralleling his course without hailing, without any sign whatsoever.

Powers' mind speculated on the feeling he had seen the rider before. It was an elusive feeling, hard to classify or weigh fairly.

"Hello!" the Texan called again, knowing before he raised his voice that there was something definitely wrong. The rider above him did not reply, merely rode along on the somewhat uneven crest. And he rode none too well.

Powers stopped his mount, and the man above did likewise. He stood silhouetted against the flawless cobalt sky—a tattered figure, silent, somehow grim. Powers' gray eyes slowly chilled.

"What in the devil!" he muttered, trying hard to pin down the elusive sense of familiarity in his mind. "I've seen you somewhere before," he muttered, "but where? And why, Dirty Shirt? Why the guardian angel act? Hey!" he called again, his voice blaring clearly in the still air. "What you playing—checkers?"

No answer.

The chill remaining in his eyes, Powers set his horse to a trot again. The man above did the same, his mount beginning the descent of the rounded hogback, taking the huge, tattered figure of its rider away from the height where it was silhouetted against the blue sky.

Obeying an impulse, Powers swung his own animal around and slapped it across the jowls with loose rein ends.

"Go get him, Bob! Go on!"

Bob stretched into a run, heading for the place where the hogback's slope became level with the gulch floor. Beyond, to the right, rose a sheer face of stone, going up to form another rounded hillock flanking the long gulch's course.

The strange rider coming down could not go up again that way—he would have either to turn to the left, toward the maze of hills behind, or veer toward Powers in the gulch. In any case, the cowboy knew that his Bob horse would overhaul him.

Bob did nobly—reaching, thrusting, gathering again. His run gained momentum. Powers sat his saddle easily;

he seemed an integral part of the animal's movements, slightly slouched, ready for the flashlight action of his draw.

The man ahead veered to the left as his mount reached level ground, and turned in the arc of a circle that carried him close to the sheer wall of stone. Powers started slightly as nearness revealed the elusive identity of his quarry.

"That sheepman, Burton, by the horns of—!"

A shock interrupted Chuck's exclamation—a forcible, extremely violent pull that jerked him out of the saddle. He had no time to draw, although some instinct swept his hands down even as the writhing riata noose dropped over his head. But the tightened coil locked his arms, wrenching his knee grip loose from his horse's sides.

His fall, heavy, jarring upon shoulders and head, stunned Powers. He tried to roll over, rise to transform the fiercely blind anger within him into action. But smothering bodies bore him down, and to make assurance doubly sure, a gun butt collided with brutal force against his head, bursting lights in his brain, sending his consciousness glimmering. A blackness engulfed his will, his blind instinct to fight, and he went limp under the pummeling bodies of men he never clearly saw.

III

The Texan came to in an evil-smelling gloom. His locked teeth stifled an impulse to groan. The pain in his head was a thing alive—a fiery throbbing of harsh sensation; his face was stiff with dried blood. And he found, as he tried to move, that his arms were locked helplessly to his sides. His whole lower body was rigid in some profuse, tightly binding coils of rope.

Powers wondered with muttered curses at the thoroughness with which he had been secured.

"Strapped like a papoose," he gritted. "They're making sure, whoever *they* are."

He raised his head, straining to get a glimpse of something or anyone.

"Hey!" he yelled forcefully. "Burton!"

There was a short interval of silence. Then the thick gloom moved; it seemed to disintegrate to his left, flow into the outline of an opening door. The bound man saw the ghostly outline of trees outside and heard the low murmuer of water somewhere beyond.

Distantly stars blinked in the sky. *Night.* In the faint outline of the doorway appeared an indistinct figure.

"Quit that," a voice snapped angrily, "or we'll jam a few rocks over yore tongue!"

The gloom hid the outrage in Powers' eyes.

"You got all the answers, fella," he commented calmly. "I've got the questions. Why don't you hombres give me a chance to talk this over? Take me out into the air. This place ain't fit for a dog."

"It's fit for the kind of dog in it now," was the cold-hearted reply. "You heard what I said. One more holler out of you, and we'll wrap up your face!"

The door slammed shut, conclusive evidence that the surly-voiced individual meant what he said. Powers did not even think of disobeying the order. He had no desire to be gagged. In the interor of that evil-smelling hut, a tight gag would suffocate him. And he had troubles enough, he decided, as his first attempt to roll over failed.

"They sure tied me!" he growled, but tried again, and this time he succeeded in tipping his rigidly trussed body. Aiding the momentum by timely shoulder heaves, he kept moving until the wall on his left stopped him. The doorway was in that wall, and doors of crude huts, generally fitted into framings with inches to spare at the bottom. After much squirming and shoulder hunching, he did find a crack in line with his eyes and peered through it, his cramped muscles aching with the strain of holding his position.

The hut was located somewhere among the low hills. From his low viewpoint Powers could see the rounded rock shoulders, a misty confusion touched by the silvering of the moon somewhere behind him, in the west. The nearer scene was as vague, though he could make out the ruddy flicker of a campfire and moving figures. Sounds came to him—voices, creek waters murmuring, and then the far bark of some prowling coyote. But all were blended into a confused faint sameness.

Relaxing, Powers stared up into the blackness. The whole affair was a bit puzzling. But his mind, clear, dynamic, trained from childhood to engage in practical thinking, did not ponder the riddle long.

How Burton and his friends had escaped from the jail in Broken Bow, and just why they had caught and confined him here, were extraneous subjects. The vital fact was that they *had* escaped, *had* trapped him, and were now holding him.

Narrowing the subject down, Powers focused his thoughts upon one problem—he was bound and he wanted to free himself. Other things could wait.

He rolled away from the wall, more to feel again the tension and nature of his bonds than to regain his former position.

"They did a good job," he muttered by habit. *"Too good. So good they slipped up on it."*

Silently then he set to work, thankful that the particular sheepmen who had caught him were not as expert at tying ropes as they were at throwing them.

The very evenness of their trussing, the rigid uniformity of it, told of a riata, or riatas, bound coil after coil around legs and hips and torso. The primary effect of such binding was discouraging—his muscles were positively clamped. But if he could successfully loosen any one coil, it meant nothing less than complete release.

Sweat started out over his muscular body. The pain in his head, momentarily forgotten, intruded again into his consciousness as his steady, straining efforts sent blood pounding through the bruised area. He could feel the slow seep of it trickling down into his eyes.

But Powers did not stop his writhing efforts.

How long he struggled without perceptible success

was a matter not considered by the angry man. The rough hair rope badly scraped the back of his hands. But he managed to jerk them free of one loop at long last. Another. And at once he felt the snug coils loosen around his thighs.

The looseness spread, and after he had removed the bulk of his arms from beneath the upper loops, the entire rope gave to his twisting, and in a matter of moments he was pulling the last strands down over his booted feet.

"Whew!" he whistled softly as he staggered to his feet. He waited until he got his breath back. "That was work! Now to get out of here!"

But getting out of the hut presented a real difficulty. The door was barred on the outside, and Powers scarcely dared to press too hard against it because of the surly-voiced guard somewhere outside.

Gluing his eye to a vertical crack between door and framing, Powers looked out again and this time plainly saw horses around the fire where just moments before had squatted the forms of men. Horses passing in front of the fire—two, three, four. Then they were gone, heading down the mountain.

A few moments later, a lone figure on foot came toward the cabin. Powers' thoughts scurried for a moment, then steadied. Burton was departing from camp with three of his men, leaving another to guard him. It was a chance to escape that seemed made to order, provided he was right that only one man had been left behind.

But Powers could not be sure this was true. How many men were with the sheepman, Burton? It was a question he could not answer. There had been only four of the sheepherders in Broken Bow. There were five, at least, in camp here.

Still, Powers' hunch that only one was staying behind to guard him—Burton and three others having left—became a conviction. And he kept remembering a rope throw that had pulled him from a running horse. This bothered him. He conceded that, being a cowman, he was biased. But he had never heard of a sheepman who could use a rope.

"Must be a joker in this woodpile," he muttered to himself. He waited for a few moments; then, flattening against the wall next to the door, he called out:

"Hey! Burton, you polecat, let me out of here!"

Footsteps sounded in the deep silence, the rasp and thud of a sliding bar. Powers smelled clean air and saw the dim form of a man, outlined head and shoulders, appear beside him.

"Didn't I tell yuh to shut—" the man began to snarl when Powers' right arm, snapping down and around, closed in a perfect, forceful stranglehold around his neck. The weight and shock of Chuck's moving body carried them both to the floor, and Powers, forced to move violently and effectively by the threat of the other's gun, was equal to the occasion. The struggle was brief, energetic and decisive. Above the straining grunts of the two men sounded the sodden smash of kunckles driven into flesh—once, again. And Powers rose from the floor alone.

"Reckon *you* won't need a gag!" he growled. About to hurry out, he considered, bent down, found a pair of inert legs and dragged the unconscious guard out after him into the clean air. Past the threshold, he shifted his grip, walked along the limp body, grasped the man by the middle and heaved him carelessly to one broad shoulder.

It was some twenty odd yards to the dying fire, its embers glowing like watchful red eyes from among a nest of rocks. In those twenty yards the guard revived. Powers could feel him stir. When finally he placed the man down, back propped against a boulder close by the fire, he had to warn him to keep quiet.

The man ceased struggling immediately upon being shown the muzzle of his own Colt.

The murmur of their talk rose over the water gurgling from the creek. The coyote barked again, somewhere in the surrounding hills.

"Now—" Powers was patient— "what are you doing with a bunch of mutton herders? You, a cowman?"

"That's my business," came the surly answer. "I told you where there's grub, my hoss, and yore Colts. You got a clean getaway ahead of you. What more do you want?"

"Plenty!" Powers snapped. His tone was metallic. "I haven't got paid yet for being nearly killed and wrapped like some skunk in that stink pen you call a hut. And I'm the kind of hombre that likes his pay and generally gets it. Where did Burton and them with him go?"

"I ain't telling," was the reply, flat and final. "And you can't make me—guns or no guns!"

Powers studied the man against the rock. He was very young—the slim, wiry type of buckaroo found in the Yellowtrail uplands. And there was hate in his voice and manner, unconcealed, sullen. Powers could literally feel the enmity emanating from the man.

"What you fools jump me for?" he shifted ground. Then, guessing: "Revenge for what happened last night at the Cactus Bar? How'd Burton get away from jail, anyhow?"

"Tunneled under the plain an' came up 'bout a mile from here," the slim cowboy sneered. "Any other questions?"

"Sure," Powers snapped back coldly. "There's other questions, and I'm getting answers to them, too!"

"Yeah?"

"Yeah. Which one of you skunks threw that rope?"

"Burton."

"You're a liar! You threw that loop yourself. No sheepherder can rope a man off a running horse that way. It's all plain now. Burton leads me close to that rock rise; you're squatting on the gulch side of it, in that greasewood, probably. When I pass you rope me—"

"Takin' three steps, movin' my arm up, back, an' jerking my wrist. We kin add details, if you want 'em. Like how much weight the rope—"

Powers balanced the Colt under the man's nose, the plain threat shutting off the flow of words.

"I'm the detail man around here, kid. You sit quiet and answer the questions—by lying, if you want. Now—which way did Burton go?"

"North!" the man answered promptly.

"Good boy!" complimented Powers. "He went north

to the SV, which is south of here, eh?"

"Go to hell!" came the impolite reply.

Powers grinned.

"You're real young yet, kid. That trick is older than these hills. Now we know Burton went south, to the SV. We also know he's got my horse, which ain't so good. Horse stealing back in Texas usually means a rope around a man's neck—"

"To hell with Texas an' everybody in it!" Powers caught the savage enmity in the young cowboy's voice again.

"Easy, easy," he soothed, a bit puzzled. "Reckon there's quite a tangle around here. Too bad I ain't got time to stop and help out. All I want, Joe Lasso, is my horse. And I'm going to get it if I have to plug Burton and every sheep nurse in this country. I'm only swapping that horse with *one* man. After I get back and give Burton a good beating for luck, I'm ambling on."

He looked off, his thoughts coming back to a futile quest, and slowly the black mood those thoughts always induced crept over him.

"Waddy, you haven't seen a big black horse with lop ears around here, have you? A great big horse, white stocking on a front leg, ears hanging?"

The man against the rock grew rigid. Powers did not

notice. He was staring into the fire, for a moment off guard, almost forgetful of where he was. But the slim cowboy abandoned the impulse to rise and leap across the separating distance. He had earlier sampled the iron strength in this man, and he knew he would have little chance.

"Yore hoss?" he asked instead, his voice a bit hoarse. "This lop-eared cayuse was yourn?"

Powers took a firm grip on himself.

"Yeah—kind of." He shrugged. "Well, *amigo*—reckon we talked enough. You gave me a pretty bad fall this afternoon, but I figger I evened that up in the hut. Now, assuming it *was* you handling the rope, it must have been somebody else who slugged me with his Colt. That makes another man I gotta lick besides Burton. And if *he* ain't riding my Bob horse, I gotta lick Bob's rider for riding him, making three. Once I go so far, I might as well pay my compliments to the whole four. You stay here, kid, and nurse 'em when they come crawling back into camp."

"You leaving me here, untied?" An incredulous suspicion was in the other's voice. "What you gonna do—ride out a way past the fire an' plug me? Give me a square break. Even a sheepherder deserves that much!"

Powers grew intent.

"What in the devil do you take me for?" he asked, frankly puzzled. Evidently he had stumbled upon some deep-rooted, bitter enmity—a fued in which the opposing interests expected no quarter from each other.

"I ain't connected with Turner," he reassured the man, guessing this might be the key to his hatred. "He's a cowman, and so am I. That's why I backed him last night. Now I'm licking Burton on my own hook. But I ain't shooting you—or anybody else—less'n I *have* to!"

He got to his feet and looked off. "Now, where did you say my Colts were?"

Ten minutes later, Powers rode off into the starlit hills, turning in the saddle to watch the still seated figure by the fire. The man lunged to his feet even as he turned and dodged into the shadows.

Powers slowly shook his head.

The man had not believed him at all.

IV

The moonlight, wan, old, a blanket of illusion, made a magic world of hill and hollow, gulch and slope. There before Chuck Powers, at the base of a long, gradual declivity, stood materialized the mental image he had formed of the SV Ranch. The fringe of cottonwoods—the half hidden house—the bunk shed and corrals—even to these details it fitted.

Powers frowned at the strange feeling that told him the SV was not a new ranch to him. Rather, he felt he had always known he would find a place like that—hills on one side—long, rolling plain behind—silence and peace and stars.

"Hell!" he disparaged with the shame of his kind for sentiment. "Reckon they're all pretty much alike—"

Again his words trailed off, and he stiffened to rigid

attention. There was indeed silence and stars around the SV, but not peace. Powers' eyes narrowed as he caught the movement again—the quick run and crouch of a man through the ghostly cottonwood fringe.

The cowboy's lips tightened. *Burton!*

Powers was off his horse's back and running now. After all, he excused his meddling, Turner was a cowman, and the four sheepherders he was after had nearly killed him. Also, they had stolen his horse.

The long grass was dry, hay-like in its crispness. It swished sharply around his boots as he ran, a small figure in that moonlight immensity of plain. Powers condoned his foolhardiness by the reflection that there was no other way to approach the ranch. And quite probably Burton and his men were so busy stalking the house they would not notice him.

Apparently his hopes fitted the facts, for he reached the creek side unmolested—a bit winded by his quick run. Crouched in the first mesquite clumps, he listened, and for a time heard nothing but the deep, utter stillness of the plains country. Then came a crackle of twigs, sharp, sudden, not twenty feet ahead of him.

Powers moved at once and expeditiously. There was nothing to gain by caution, when every man on the ranch beyond the creek was a friend. Also, caution was useful in serious cases, and Powers could not in this case work up the proper mood. He wanted to scare the sheepmen away, not kill any one of them.

So he broke from cover with considerable noise, adding a wild yell for effect. The spirit of the thing grew on him as he saw three figures close to the house scurry away like rabbits, causing him to draw his Colts and fire away at the serene, aloof stars. His actions were careless of his personal safety, for like most cowmen, he had nothing but contempt for sheepherders when it came to the use of firearms.

He received a painful surprise. Hardly had he begun his run toward the creek when a bullet struck him high up in the left arm, and he felt a searing pain that stiffened him momentarily. Instinct cut down his blazing Colts to spit his reply to the gun flashes on his left—and his regret was real and genuine when the hammers began to click over empty cartridge cases. Dropping down on his knees, he let his left Colt slide from numb fingers, transferred the other to their feeble grip and deftly began picking new shells from his belt with a normal right hand.

"Darn fool!" he berated himself. "Running out like some kid at a carnival! And *him,* a sheepman, letting drive to get me! All I wanted to do was scare him off."

His voice hardened. "Hope I winged one of the skunks, anyway!"

The bushes to his left, from which had come the unexpected shots, were a motionless black clump in the moonlight. The three men he had frightened away from the house were nowhere to be seen. Beyond, in the ranch yard, were signs of activity—running forms— the open, yellow-lighted square of the bunkhouse door.

"This way!" called Powers, and began to approach the mesquite clump he had fired into, a reloaded Colt balanced in his right hand. "This way!" His voice dropped sharply as a low, stifled groan came to his ears. Parting the bushes, he made out a dark form sprawled behind them.

"So I did get one of you!" he growled. "Served you right—though I'm kinda sorry. Hey!" he yelled again. "Turner—this way!"

Turner and the SV cowboys made much of Powers in the following hour. The Texan said little, revolving a puzzle in his mind. The man his snap shots had wounded was in critical condition—the chances were even that he would die. He lay in Sandra Vaughn's room, his dirty form sprawled over the bedspread, while the girl, working deftly with water and bandages, took

care of him. She had previously bandaged Powers'
wounded arm and thereby repaid him with interest for
the way it hurt.

The cowboys, a half-dozen slim, hard-faced riding
men, talked in the living room, occasionally coming to
the inner door to make remarks or ask questions. Turner
stood by Powers' side, both watching the girl wash and
bind the ugly gunshot wounds in the sheepman's chest.

"They're high up," she kept repeating hopefully.
"One is too high to have hurt the lung. Oh, I hope he
doesn't die—I hope Wills finds Doctor Paine sober."

"Well—" Turner shrugged— "he brought it on himself, Sandra."

He turned to Powers. "You say you came out yelling, shooting in the air? And he shot you?"

"Yeah," Powers answered. But the puzzle grew in
his mind. He was feeling decidedly uncomfortable at
the thought of the sheepman dying.

"I'm feeling bad about the whole thing," he con-
fessed frankly. "He shot at me first, and I don't regret
shooting back. But—"

The girl straightened, looking up at him through a
tumble of disarrayed brown hair.

"We understand, Mr. Powers. Joe is that way himself—never shoots until he has to, then regrets it. But

what are we to do?"

She came over to them, and Powers, looking at her earnest, troubled face, knew that Joe Turner was a very lucky man.

"Nobody knows or understands what I've been through," she continued. "I hate to see men fight—I'm afraid of blood—and here we are, harassed by these men—"

"Just what have they got against you?" Powers asked Turner. His gaze was on the unconscious sheepman as he asked the question—his thoughts were back by a campfire in the hills.

"I cleaned out a pretty rustling game of theirs—that's what," explained Turner.

Powers looked interested. "Cleaned them out, eh?"

"Sure. That's how I come to get a job as foreman here. I rode up this way from Texas a few months back—looking for work in a new country. I found things kinda different here in the Yellowtails. They haven't got much use for guns, and sheepherders and cowmen drink side by side in the local bars. Like a single saddle cinch, that don't make sense to me. But I needed money, and so I bunked with this outfit. Oh, it wasn't *this* outfit then; just a half-dozen sleepy waddies—buckaroos they called themselves—who trusted the whole world. Said they never had trouble. Seems like I couldn't believe it, but they said so—"

"We hadn't, Joe," the girl put in seriously. "We really had not been bothered at all for years."

Turner frowned.

"Well—it certainly started heavy. I wasn't here a month when I had to shoot a man. I'd been riding the south line, up near the hills, and missing cows. Mavericks were so cussed scarce I began to think someone else was collecting them; and following a hunch south, I saw it proved. There's a pocket in the hills about ten miles south and west of here—hard to find. Ground around is rocky and leaves no hoof marks. I rode into it by luck and surprised a man branding SV stock.

"We had words. He went for his Colt, and I shot him. Come to find out he was a Box Circle rider." Turner shrugged. "That's when the trouble started. His mates didn't believe he was rustling, even after it was proved."

Powers dipped into his pockets for the makings. Turner supplied the match. The girl gazed back at the man on the bed, then turned her attention to the story she had heard at least a score of times—the story which proved Joe Turner to be a man among men. Two of the cowboys, coming to the doorway for a glance within, remained, listening attentively to what Joe Turner was recalling.

"I reckon this feller wasn't branding that SV maverick with a Box Circle iron, was he?" Powers asked idly.

"Heck, no!" Turner shook his head decisively. "I ain't ever accused the Box Circle of rustling. It's too big a ranch for that. And Tommy Boyd, their foreman, is as square as they come. But he is kinda thick. Claims this feller I shot—Drake—was his best rider, and honest. Well—mebbe he was a good puncher for them, but he wasn't honest! I caught him with that running iron in his hand—caught him dead to rights. And I shot him because he was trying to kill me. But he had a brother working for Boyd—Al Drake—who's swore to get me for that shooting. Others sided with him on the same claim, but I'm figgering all of them hotheads was in on the rustling. It was war after that. I had to shoot a couple of others who tried to get me in town, and I gave them fair warning I'd shoot any of them I saw riding SV range."

He paused and looked at the girl bending over the wounded man on the bed. "The hands working for the SV then weren't much help, so I sent back to Texas for some real punchers. After the dust settled, the SV was boss ranch in this section."

He eyed Powers frankly. "Now I ask you, Chuck—leaving it up to yore judgment as a square man and a Texan yoreself—they held it against me that I was a stranger and pretty handy with a gun. But right is right and wrong is wrong, ain't it? I'm sorry, of course, that Boyd was thick-headed about it, but I couldn't help it—"

"I was sorry, too, Mr. Powers," the girl interjected. "My father thought the world of Tommy Boyd. So did I. Perhaps that was one cause of the bitter feeling that came afterward. I don't like to believe it, of course, but—"

"I understand," Powers said slowly. "Tommy was in love with you, and Joe here beat him out. So Turner was wrong, no matter what he did."

Her eyes laughed up at him, pleased.

"You're older than you look, Mr. Powers."

"Please," Powers said a bit gruffly, "don't call me Mister. Makes me feel stiff like. Chuck's my name, even when I look sad."

"Chuck." Her eyes laughed again, then sobered. "We thank you, Chuck—again."

"So do I, Chuck," Turner put in a bit brusquely. "That's twice you broke up Burton's game. You've put yourself in a lot of trouble, for me—"

"That's what I'm puzzling over," Powers admitted frankly. "Your story's about a range war between the Box Circle and this ranch. Where does Burton, the sheepman, come in?"

Turner shrugged, looking over to the wounded man on the bed.

"Just something that grew out of the first trouble," he said, and Powers sensed more than pleasant forcefulness in the man's voice—heard the elusive, intangible ring of real regret.

"Burton had a boy, about ten years old. He was shot in one of our fights with the Box Circle punchers by mistake."

Powers saw the girl pale; trouble clouded her face.

"That sheepman went crazy over it," Turner continued. "Wanted revenge. He wouldn't leave the sheriff alone, although nobody knew for sure if it was an SV or Box Circle bullet that killed him. Burton took his sheep down from the hills onto our range, claiming he had the right to everything we owned—"

"What about what he said you did—in the saloon? Something about driving his sheep over a cliff."

"Never did it!" Turner said after a moment's hesitation. "I haven't bothered Burton at all, off our land."

"Of course not!" Sandra said earnestly. "Joe could never do a thing like that. Nor could any of the hired men on this ranch. But we're talking too much," she added noticing a tired look about Powers' eyes. "We've forgotten that Chuck is hurt and should be kept quiet for a few days." She made a gesture toward another part of the house. "You'll sleep in father's room, Chuck—"

"What about you, Sandra?" Turner asked.

"Oh, I'll probably not be able to sleep at all tonight. Don't you worry, Joe—you know how strong I am. Besides, Chuck is our guest and must be made comfortable." She smiled. "Wyoming hospitality, you know."

"Of course, Chuck," Turner said curtly, "make yoreself at home."

Turner had his bad points, the Texan decided during a sleepless night. He was a jealous man, and harder than he appeared, at least when the girl was around. In fact, Powers reflected restlessly, Joe Turner was a very dangerous man whose quiet manner and soft talk were a shield, and a mirror image which he held up for Sandra Vaughn to view.

Powers' thoughts drifted to the young cowman he had left behind in the hills. Harry Drake's brother Al, most probably. No wonder he had hated Chuck, feeling as he must have that he was just another Texan come up the trail to join Turner.

The girl bothered him the most. He hardly knew her, and he would be riding on as soon as his arm healed. He had no reason to stick around, to get embroiled in a range war in which he felt no real allegiance to either side.

It was a mess.

V

Chuck Powers stayed two weeks at the SV Ranch. His arm wound healed slowly, yet the fact caused him little impatience, so little that he came to realize why and faced his problem squarely.

The two weeks had seemed to flow by—days and nights with a new interest—lounging, lazy hours by the corral fence watching a somewhat strange-acting outfit as it drifted in or out of the ranch in pairs or in groups or singly. He had never worked on a ranch in which the hired hands seemed to do pretty much as they pleased. He could understand the girl not taking charge, but Joe Turner, her foreman and the man she planned to marry, seemed to run his riders with a loose hand, which was a far departure from the usual run of Texas ramrods.

Still, Chuck gave it little more than passing thought.

He spent his recuperating days riding over the rolling plain along the edge of the hills south of the ranch—riding with Sandra Vaughn. It took two weeks for his arm to heal. Toward the end certain things became plain to him, and Powers began to regret the whole affair.

It was late afternoon of a hot, sultry day when he looked frankly at the problem. He had come in from his daily ride with Sandra, who was now talking to Turner by the side of the ranch house. They were getting married next month, the girl had said a few hours before, her voice a bit hesitant.

Relaxing in the dry, fragrant grass close to the bunkhouse, Powers watched the hill tumble to the west with hard and mocking eyes. From the jagged horizon his gaze returned to the man and woman by the house.

"I'm due to ramble on again, that's all. Hell!" he swore in self-contempt. "What a fool! Come riding through those hills one night aiming to punch a few skunks' noses and get back my horse. There's a house and a bunk shed and a corral, all silver in the moonlight. There's a creek and trees and stars and quiet. There's everything a fool thinks about when he ain't got anything else to think about. There's even the girl—just like he's always pictured her. The fool gets himself shot, and they make him hang around. Everything is nice—Chuck here and Chuck there—Chuck, come riding with me. But what's the decent thing to do now? Get out," he answered himself savagely, his lips curling a bit. "I've been forgetting a lot of things—forgetting Dad's grave back in Texas—forgetting the promise I made myself—not even looking to square my debts to the polecats who jumped me here!"

He suddenly rose, grateful that his left arm, which he used in helping himself up, scarcely twinged. "Reckon my stay is over," he muttered thankfully, moving toward Turner and the girl. "It's time I took one of Joe's hints and moved. Sunset—a good time to fog out—"

Joe Turner drew a mask of pleasantness over his visage as Powers approached and a cold disapproval troubled the newly arrived Texan. After all, Turner had the winning hand here—the only possible winning hand in the game—and there should be no reason for his hidden enmity. But Powers had no illusions about the man. The good-looking foreman whose life he had saved had grown to hate him during the interval of his stay at the SV Ranch.

"Chuck—" the girl's tone grew animated as the Texan neared— "it took you a long time to corral the horses."

"Aw—I stopped by the bunkhouse," Powers replied, repressing a desire to frown. The girl was too pretty and her eyes altogether too friendly. "I was thinking, Miss Sandra—like a lazy man regretting my vacation is over."

"Over?" She did not understand. Powers saw a vague uneasiness come to her eyes as he explained why he had to leave.

"I haven't got my Bob horse back yet," he summed up, "and while I've given up on the idea of punching Burton's nose, I still want that cayuse. So I'm going after him. In the meantime, I'm thanking you all for my free room and board, and—" he forced himself to keep his voice light— "wishing you and Joe all the happiness you deserve."

Sandra Vaughn saw the world change, the fading sunlight grow cold.

"You're going away?" She asked it as though the thing were beyond imagining. "Why?" Then reason showed her the strangeness of her attitude and she quickly composed herself. "Oh, we're really sorry, Chuck, to see you go."

"Sure are," lied Turner, the mask for the moment gone from his eyes. Powers saw hate in them, plain and ugly—an enmity that slowly chilled him.

"We're sure sorry you're going, Powers," the foreman continued, and even the girl noticed the strain in his voice. "Too bad you can't stay for the wedding."

A level hardness crept into Powers' eyes—a contemptuous reaction to what he sensed in Turner. The foreman seemed a different man on closer acquaintance. And he was jealous. The Texan wondered why luck always seemed to go with fools.

"Yeah, too bad," he concluded, his tone conveying finality. "But I got that Bob horse to find. So I'm saying goodbye, Miss Sandra—"

"You be careful, Chuck."

Another man would have caught the serious concern in her voice. Turner caught it. But Powers scarcely heard. He even welcomed the interruption which saved him from a reply.

The rider, loping around the bunkhouse, was asking for Joe Turner.

Powers' gaze took in a big roan horse, a spare, bony figure topping the saddle, with a flowing mustache and a badge pinned to an open black vest. The whole ensemble formed a personality—and fitted the authoritative voice.

"You're Turner?" The roan's rider looked sharply at the foreman; then: "You got a cowboy up here—

Texas hand who helped you out in a squabble with Luke Burton a while back?"

Powers stepped forward.

"I'm the hombre, Deputy—"

A pair of keen, cold eyes looked Powers over.

"Yeah. Well, get yourself a horse. The law wants to talk to you."

Exultation flickered up through the surprise in Joe Turner's eyes. The girl started.

"The law? Why, that's preposterous!" She stood looking from Powers to the hard-faced man waiting on the roan horse.

Powers shrugged.

"I must have done somethin," he guessed. Then, eyeing the lawman: "Say, that sheepherder didn't die, did he? Are you Sheriff Orrins?"

"No. I'm Sheriff Orrins' new deputy, the last resort of a peaceful peace officer. Borden's my name. And I'm warning you right off—no monkey shines. I'm nothing like Sheriff Orrins or the deputies he's had. When I'm ordered to take a man in he comes in—sometimes feet first!"

"Yeah?" Powers let a grin slide around his lips. "No need of that at all in my case, Deputy. I'm real gentle, and glad of the company back to town. I was going in anyway."

He turned to Turner and the girl. "Well, luck to both of you. Can I use that horse I've been riding, Miss Sandra? One of your hands can pick him up in town."

A few minutes later Deputy Lou Borden, one-time marshal of Dodge City, rode away from the SV with his prisoner, who was not thinking of the law at all, but of a girl's strangely disturbing manner of parting from friends.

He did not look back, having learned that a break was best left clean, and useless memories given as little to feed upon as possible. And after a time the puzzle of the law wanting him began to intrude into the Texan's thoughts, forcing out vague regrets at what he had missed in life.

"So you're Deputy Borden?" he broke the ice, somehow feeling at home with the bony, mustached man. "And you're not like the sheriff. What's the matter with the sheriff?"

Their horses were loping along a twilit trail—their pounding and pushing of hoofs making monotonous sounds in the gathering dusk.

"You know what's the matter with him, I reckon. He's old and not too anxious to get shot up. So he passes up the dangerous assignments, like going after

Texas gunslingers—"

"Gunslinger!" Powers stared at him.

"Maybe a little rustling on the side, too," Borden said. His voice was even, and Powers couldn't tell if he was kidding or if he meant it.

"Look, Deputy—you've got me wrong," Chuck said. "I'm just a stranger up here, rambling on. Only thing I did was shoot that sheepherder who was trying to ambush Joe Turner. And I only shot him in self-defense!"

"Nice story," the deputy commented coldly. "We'll hear the rest of it in the sheriff's office!"

VI

Broken Bow was in full swing of its evening revelry when Powers and Orrins' new deputy rode in.

"Box Circle boys spending their pay," Lou Borden explained as they loped past the Cactus Bar. The murmur of talk and laughter faded, rose again in lesser volume each time they passed a saloon. "The boys rode in with their foreman, Boyd—he's waiting in Sheriff Orrins' office right now, just across the street there. We'll let the horses stand," the deputy added easily. "They won't keep you long."

Powers dismounted and saw a dark square building close to the end of town. It appeared to be a bit more solidly built than the ragtag false fronts making up most of Broken Bow's main street.

As he approached the door he could see cracks of

light coming through the lower windows, shining through drawn curtains.

"Regular mystery," he remarked dryly. "The law's waiting for a badman from Texas, now entering."

Lou Borden did not appear amused.

Chuck opened the door and stepped into a narrow, dark hallway. He stopped abruptly, a faint warning crinkling his back muscles.

"You take the trail, Deputy," he said quietly. "I'm lost."

Borden knocked on a side door and pushed through at the gruff, "Come on in!"

Powers calmly stepped inside behind the deputy. He found himself in a large lamplit room—a long, solid desk across its end. An older man with a sheriff's badge was seated behind it; another man was at its head, tipped back in his chair, smoking.

Two other men stood by the wall on Powers' left, and interest took the place of uneasy amusement in Chuck's eyes. *Burton and one of his herders!*

Across the room, straddling a chair, was yet another individual, and Powers' carelessness passed entirely from him.

He had last seen that man, weeks before, seated by a campfire in the hills, dodging into the shadows as he turned in the saddle while riding away. Parts of stories connected in Powers' mind. Al Drake, brother of the rustler Joe Turner had shot up in the hills behind the SV.

Sheriff Orrins, a bit portly, heavy of jowl and throat, blinked weak eyes at the entrants and rose.

"Good work, Lou," he complimented, "good work. I guess you know what you're talking about."

"Said I'd bring him in without help, didn't I?" Borden's voice held amusement. "And I want you gents to notice I left him his Colts, just to make him feel natural."

The sheriff looked a bit uneasy. Burton scowled. The man at the desk did not move. Al Drake, on the right, straddling the chair, smiled thinly.

"He couldn't bust out of here with a Gatling gun," he observed. "Mike's buddies are out there, with some of Tommy's boys. They waited for you to ride in, Borden; we wanted to make sure of him."

Powers turned to Al Drake, his face hard. Mike was the name of the bushwhacker he had shot at the SV.

The sheriff said not too confidently: "You better sit down, Mr. Powers—"

Chuck ignored the lawman's order.

"That feller, Mike?" he asked Drake. "Did he pull

through?"

Drake did not answer him; enmity was naked and bitter in his gaze.

Sheriff Orrins answered for him. "Yes," he said, "Mike's recovering. But never mind him, Powers—" He turned to Drake. "And you, Al—don't you think of starting any trouble here."

Al shrugged, his eyes judging Powers, sneering.

Orrins held out a hand to Powers. "Just to make sure, let me have your guns—"

Powers' gray eyes froze. He underwent a complete metamorphosis—a change so palpable that the hardened deputy, Lou Borden, felt it and gazed at the Texan with new interest. Borden had a gift of sensing the characters of men, and it told him things about Powers now. The deputy's gaze went slowly to Drake, who was watching, tensed in his chair.

"Yeah—reckon you'd better, Powers," Borden said, backing up the sheriff's request. He laid a hand on his gun butt as he talked. "Best for all of us that way."

Powers' better judgment took over. The fire went out of his gaze as he nodded slowly. "All right," he said thickly, "if it'll make things easier. . . ."

Lou Borden eased his hand away from his gun and relaxed, as did every other man in that room. The sheepherder beside Burton breathed an audible sigh of relief. Without exactly understanding its nature, all knew that a crisis had been passed.

Slowly Powers drew out the two plain flare butt .45's and laid them on the long table. In the lamp glow, the long gun barrels glinted faintly. Borden's eyes dwelt on the wood butts worn to shiny blackness.

"I'm breaking a promise, Sheriff," Powers said, "just to help the law. Seven—no, near eight months ago I sheathed these guns, promising myself to sleep with them, nurse them, remember them before everything else, until I found the man I was trailing. It's hard to put them aside now."

"What's all this, Sheriff?" snapped Drake from his chair. "When are we gonna talk business?"

"Right now," replied Sheriff Orrins with more confidence. Borden settled into a chair beside Powers. "Sit down, Powers," he said, his eyes hard now, judging.

The sheriff proceeded to put his questions in order in a manner which surprised Borden, whose opinion of his superior was not flattering. The unusual occasion, he thought, had stirred Orrins' usually dull mind.

"From what you've been telling us," Sheriff Orrins said to Powers, "you're not connected with Joe Turner in any way. You didn't know Turner back in Texas?"

"No!" Powers snapped. "I never saw Joe Turner until the night I rode into Broken Bow. Stopped in at the Cactus Bar for a meal and a bunk and ran into Burton there, having trouble with Turner. Turner talked Texas—he was a cowman, I could *tell* that right off—and there was four grown men to one. So I horned in, and—" his tone hardened— "I'd do it again on that basis. But right now I'm beginning to be sorry I did horn in—"

"All right," Borden interrupted dryly. "You say you're not connected with Turner. You helped him because he was a cattleman and a Texan. But you say you're sorry, maybe, you did horn in. Why?"

Powers did not reply at once. The question was first judged fairly, then fairly answered.

"In some ways I am. But the reason I'm sorry hasn't got a thing to do with any law. Outside of plugging Mike, I got no argument with the law."

"How about the big black horse with the lop ears?" Drake rasped, rising from his chair. "Maybe you're not in with Joe Turner—*just maybe!* But one question, damn it! And I want a straight answer, you Texas killer—was that stud your horse?"

"Easy, Drake!" Borden growled, his nerves going taut. Powers' eyes had blazed again. The little twitch of his shoulders meant things to the deputy, who mentally gave thanks that Sheriff Orrins had asked for Powers' guns.

"Sit down, Powers," he requested in a calmer tone. "You—Drake—one more break like that, and I'll bounce you out of here! Burton, too! Any of you!"

"Yes!" Sheriff Orrins tried to assume the proper tone. "We'll have no hotheaded arguments in here. You gonna keep quiet, Drake?"

Al Drake sat down slowly, watching the Texan like a hawk. Slowly Powers took a grip on his blind rage.

"I'm asking one thing, too," he said, his voice strained. "Shuffle all the riddles you want to—take your time about them, all of you. You got your troubles to settle. You think I'm mixed up in them. Well, I ain't. But one thing we are going to find out before I answer another question—what's the horse with the lop ears got to do with all of this? Anybody here ever *see* that horse?"

"Me," Drake said evenly, ignoring the sheriff's warning.

"Me, too." The man at the desk spoke for the first time. His tipped-back chair thudded down, and through the rising film of cigaret smoke he regarded Powers.

"My name's Tommy Boyd. Ramrod at the Box Circle.

The black stud with the lop ears is getting fat up at the ranch right now." His eyes narrowed. "Texas—what we'd all like to know is this: Is that horse *yourn?*"

"You got that horse up at your place?" In a dead silence the Texan rose. "*Who rode him up there?*"

"Say—say," Sheriff Orrins growled, a note of alarm in his voice. "No need to—"

"Who rode that horse?" Powers said harshly, overriding the sheriff. "I've got to know!"

A puzzled suspicion glinted in Al Drake's eyes.

"I rode him up to the Box Circle," he said flatly. "I found him in that draw where you left him, after killing one of Burton's men!"

"Hold it right there!" Powers blazed. "Reckon we are all tangled, gents! And maybe explanations could clear things. But I'm not in the explaining mood right now. Law or no law—I'm not telling some things until I finish my business with the man who rode that horse *before* Drake found him. *I* ain't that man. If you've got any sense at all, you oughta see that. I *want* the man who rode him. Now," he said gratingly, facing Drake, "just where did you find that black stallion?"

Drake said harshly: "To hell with you, Texas!"

He turned to Borden, who put a hand on his arm, pulling him back.

"How do we know, Deputy, that he ain't mixed up with that murdering polecat on the SV? Just because *he* says so? Look at the evidence! He backs Turner in an argument with Burton—then, very convenient, he shoots one of Burton's men right at Turner's door. And what's he doing when you rode out to get him? Why, he's living it up, pretty as you please, with Turner and the rest of them. Borden—*look at it!* They're both from Texas. Turner's imported other gunmen from Texas. What's so *different* about him?"

"What I think is *my* business!" Borden snapped. "Now you sit back and hold your tongue, Drake! Remember, the law's been easy on you—maybe because the sheriff here knows all of you personally. And I reckon he knew your brother Harry."

He turned to the scowling sheepman. "And he remembers your wife, Burton—and your boy. That makes it all bad—for the law's the law. You're sure Al Drake's brother wasn't rustling SV beef when Turner rode up to him in the hills—but Turner's got proof. There was the small holding corral, the running iron, the twenty head of stock rebranded Single R. It was small-scale rustling, and if Harry Drake wasn't doing it, whoever it was is still free, and Turner brought in the wrong man, that's all. But you got nothing except ideas to say so—

and you can't go gunning for a man just because of ideas—"

He watched Al Drake closely as he finished.

"No?" Harry's brother sneered the word. "Well, you try and stop me, Deputy! I'm getting Joe Turner for killing my brother, and I'm telling it out loud and clear that I ain't calling him in an even break. I ain't got a dog's chance that way. Harry didn't, and Harry's draw was five times faster'n mine. No, I won't kill Turner in an even shootout—but I'll get him some way! No, I won't pot-shoot him!" he replied with angry contempt to the deputy's cold question. "I ain't the skunk he is! But I'll get him somehow!"

"You're talking foolish, Al," Sheriff Orrins said regretfully. "Borden's right. All you and Burton have are ideas and suspicions. And this don't give you the right to keep up this feud with Turner. Just look at it this way. If Mike had died, the law couldn't hold Powers for it. Mike was on somebody else's land, and he wasn't there for his health. That's where Turner's right and you fellers wrong. I haven't heard of Turner going gunning for any of you boys yet. He's defending SV stock and SV ground, and he has the right to call on me and Borden here to back him up. Look," he said placatingly, "take it easy. Way you're going about it, you're just making a mess of things—"

"How about my sheep?" Burton rasped. "Somebody ran them over the cliff, not more than three days after I warned Turner to leave the country and he told me I was leaving first. Don't the law back me there? That ain't SV ground, out there past Shadow Lake!"

Borden said flatly: "I'm looking into it. In the meantime—"

"Turner keeps on doing just as he pleases!" Drake snapped. "Well, I ain't waiting. Neither is Burton." He turned to Powers. "And we're starting with him, Borden. Far as I'm concerned, he's a Texan, and a Turner man, and—"

Powers shoved Borden into Drake, sending them both tumbling over Al's chair. He snatched up his guns, thumbing back the hammers. His eyes were bleak, deadly.

"Anybody else here want to start with me?"

No one moved.

"All right," he said, his voice shaking, "I've waited here, listening to your troubles, taking your accusations. But I never did get an answer to what is most important to me! *Who was the man who rode the black horse before Drake found him?*"

No one answered him—maybe no one knew.

"Well, I was aiming to amble on," he said bitterly. "Almost gave up trying to find him. But now I know that man is here, somewhere! And I'll find him!"

He backed slowly to the door. "Don't anybody be in a rush," he warned. "I scare easy."

He was on his horse and headed out of town, for the dark, distant hills, before anyone in the room moved.

VII

Deputy Lou Borden eyed the angry men in the room, the gun in his hand backing his command.

"No one's leaving here until I say so!"

Al Drake quivered with rage, "He's getting away, Deputy! That killer'll be out of the country by morning!"

"I don't think so!" Lou snapped.

Al started to shove past him, and the deputy jammed the muzzle of his gun into the young cowboy's stomach.

"Don't push me, kid!"

Al stopped, biting his lips. He ran his gaze to his foreman, Boyd, angry, appealing for help. Boyd shrugged, indicating there was nothing he could do.

"Now sit down and listen to me!" Lou snapped. He shoved Drake back into his chair and turned, eying the others, his eyes hard, unrelenting.

The sheepman, Burton, said bitterly: "Hell, Deppity, you'd think we're the ones who are—"

"Shut up!" Lou cut him off. His voice was grim. "I'll do the talking here!"

Burton stiffened. His herder, a lanky, pale-eyed man named Cy, shifted uneasily. Tommy Boyd frowned.

Sheriff Orrins said placatingly: "Now, now, Lou, these are friends of mine. You can't—"

"That's what's wrong," Borden said coldly. "When the law starts taking sides, we're in trouble, friends or no friends!"

Sheriff Orrins scowled. "I think you're forgetting something, Lou. You're my deputy, not my boss!"

Lou's left hand reached up to his badge. "Any time you want to do without me," he said curtly, "you just say the word."

"I didn't mean that, Lou." Orrins mopped his round face with his handkerchief. "I reckon we're all upset." He looked around at the others. "Lou's right. I've been too easy on you. From now on, keep away from the SV Ranch and Joe Turner. We'll take care of the law here—"

Al Drake jerked to his feet. I'll keep away from the Vaughn ranch," he said grimly, "but not from Joe Turner. And if Turner's Texas friend, Powers, is still around, I'll be looking for him, too!"

Lou said flatly: "I'm repeating my order, Drake! You stay clear of Turner, or I'll jail you right now!"

Drake licked his lips, his eyes defiant.

Boyd said quickly: "I'll keep Al in line, Lou." He came to his feet, a big, amiable man disturbed by all this. "I've been trying to keep out of trouble with the SV But now—" his tone hardened— "because of Joe Turner, I can't. I know what all this trouble must be doing to Sandra Vaughn." He shook his head. "Things were different when her father was alive. We never had any trouble in the Basin until Turner arrived. Now—" he scowled— "we're losing beef. I've got some boys making a tally count now; won't know how much we've lost until they're through. Sure, I know Turner's claiming the same thing—that he's losing SV beef. Could be we're dealing with a clever band of rustlers who've moved in on us—"

"The trouble started when Turner took over at the SV," Drake said harshly. "That's enough for me."

"I ran my sheep in the hills past Shadow Lake," Burton put in, his voice thick with suppressed rage. "Nobody bothered me. We got along well enough, considering this was cattle country; then Joe Turner showed up. When I useta come to town here I was *'Mister* Burton,' just like anybody else; not *'that damn sheepherder'!* Maybe that's just Texas talk, Deppity, but I don't like it!'' His face darkened. "I'll stay away from the SV all right—but some day I'll find the man who killed my boy; the same man who rode that lop-eared black stud horse into the Basin and turned him loose after. And I'll not be waiting for the law then!''

He pushed angrily by Borden, walking to the door. "Cattlemen stick by cattlemen in this country, and Texans side with Texans. Me, I'm just a dumb sheepherder—''

Boyd said heavily: "Now, Luke, we've been getting along fine—''

"Yeah—just as long as I kept on my side of the Shadow Lake country,'' Burton said harshly. "Somebody ran three hundred head of my sheep over a cliff, but I didn't notice anybody here losing any sleep over it. Now, if it had been Box Circle beef—''

Boyd's face flushed angrily. "You've no right to say that, Luke!''

"The hell I haven't!'' Burton snarled. "I sat here an' listened to you talk; nobody said anything about my troubles. Just the SV and Joe Turner and the Box Circle! Well, the devil with all of you! And one more thing! I've got the horse of that Texan, Joe Turner's friend—and I hear Powers is going to come looking for him. Well, I've got a thirty-thirty up at the camp I keep for wolves."

He turned to Borden. "You want to stop me, you better do it right now, Deputy, with that gun yo're so handy with!"

Lou eyed the angry man, admiration in his eyes for Burton.

"Go back to your camp and stay put for a while," he said mildly enough. "Just think things over a bit. That's all I ask, Burton."

Burton said harshly: "Yeah, I'll think things over. But it'll still come out to the same thing. Deppity— Joe Turner and his Texas gunslinger—Powers!"

He motioned to the lanky man waiting by the wall. "Come on, Cy. Let's get out of here!"

Al Drake slowly pushed himself up from the chair. "Well, looks like the parley's over. We didn't find out much, an' we wound up lettin' Powers get away." He smiled bitterly. "Well, what the devil!" He looked at his foreman. "I'm ridin' back to the ranch, Mr. Boyd. That is—" he turned to Borden— "if *you* don't mind, Deppity?"

There was a challenge in his voice.

Borden shrugged. "Just remember—first time you go gunning for Turner, or any of the SV hands, I'll slap you in jail!"

Al said with false pleasantness, "Oh, I'll be a good boy, Deputy." He went to the door, paused.

"Always heard Texans stuck together. And you are from Texas, ain't you, Borden?"

Borden's jaw hardened. He nodded.

"Well, looks like Joe Turner's got everything his way now," Drake said quietly. "He's turned the old Vaughn ranch into a Texas spread, got a lawman from Texas on his side, an'—"

"Cut that out, Al!" Boyd's sharp voice stopped him. "Get back to the ranch and stay there!"

Al Drake took a deep breath. "Sure. Not much else I can do. My brother's dead. Like Burton said, 'Who cares?'" He shoved his hat back from his forehead, his eyes hard, bitter. "But just in case, Deppity, I'm keeping *my* rifle oiled, too!"

After he had gone, Tommy Boyd said heavily: "He's just a kid, Lou. He's looked up to his brother ever since their folks died." He was silent for a moment, thinking of what had happened since.

"I don't like the way things are going, either, Lou. Turner's fired all the old hands and brought in men from Texas. Then this gunslinger friend of his shows up—"

"I'm not so sure he's a friend of Turner's," Borden cut in. He frowned, thinking back. "Powers was real friendly all the way in from the ranch. He didn't seem concerned at all, not until he got here and somebody mentioned the lop-eared black horse."

"I've got that horse on my ranch," Boyd said. "Al found him wandering around loose 'bout a month or so ago. Got a Line O brand on him." Boyd shook his head. "No spread using that iron in this part of the country—"

Orrins made a gesture of irritability. "What's the sense talking about Powers? Like Al said, he'll be way out of the country by morning."

"I don't think so," Borden replied thoughtfully. He extracted a slim black cheroot from his vest pocket and stuck it in a corner of his mouth.

"Well, let's turn in. I got some riding to do in the morning."

VIII

Just before Burton and his herder, Cy, left the meeting in the sheriff's office, a man slipped out of the Cactus Bar and wandered toward the law building. He was a tall, slender man, his age hidden behind a poker face and shrewd knowing eyes. He had arrived in town a week ago, on a through stage, had stopped for a friendly game of poker, listened to idle talk in the saloon, and with a carelessness that somehow did not appear to be part of his nature, had forgotten to be on hand when the stage rolled on.

So he hung around in Broken Bow, his only visible means of support his winnings at the poker table.

He gave his name casually as Reno Smith, and as casually spent his days. He seldom won too much, but he won steadily and avoided trying to give the impression he could have won more. He dressed in town clothes, well cut but a trifle shabby now. He wore a gun in a shoulder holster, but it was unobtrusive, and no one knew how well he could use it, or if he ever had. He was not a quarrelsome man. He told no tall tales, never spoke of where he was from, and smiled readily enough, although one could tell he was not a laughing man.

It was a slow night at the poker table, and besides, he had won his daily quota. He had come out earlier in the evening for a smoke, and the riders pulling up in front of the sheriff's office had attracted his attention.

It was a warm night, with most of the windows open. Maybe, he thought, he could hear something of importance.

He reached the side of the building, moving with the easy walk of a man on a stroll. He paused to light a cigaret, his ears tuned to angry voices he could hear inside. But either the windows were closed, or the walls were muting the voices. He could not make out what was being said, other than there was anger in it. For a moment he had the impulse to slip around to the side of the building, then thought better of it.

Horses stamped restlessly at the tie bar in front of the building. He moved closer to them, his gaze running casually over the brands. It was an old, acquired habit. He stiffened.

The big bay horse on the off side of the rail struck a chord of recognition, yet he knew it could not be the same one he remembered. He moved closer and ran his hand down the animal's rump. It was a light runner with *no brand,* and now he knew!

It's a long way from Texas, he thought. He chuckled coldly. "Looks like I found a way to cut myself in on whatever it is the Kid's got cooking up here."

He was moving back when he heard a door slam inside the building. He ducked into the shadows by the corner of the building and watched as Burton and his man, Cy, emerged.

Burton stopped by the big bay and looked off into the night, anger still riding him. He ran his hand over the bay's shoulder. "Reckon he missed him in the dark, being in a hurry," he said to Cy. "But he told Al he'd come after me; he wants his horse back." He grinned bitterly, his eyes cloudy with frustration. "I want him to come, Cy; only this time I'll be waiting for him—with a gun!"

He mounted the bay and pulled away from the hitchrack. Cy mounted his cayuse and fell in beside him. Neither man rode gracefully, but they rode determinedly.

Reno Smith watched them head out of town. He would have liked to know what the meeting was all about, but it was the bay horse that excited him.

He was halfway back to the Cactus Bar when more noise from the sheriff's office stopped him. He saw Al Drake step outside, mount his horse and go galloping up the street.

Reno knuckled his jaw thoughtfully.

It was time, he thought, to pay the Rio Kid a visit.

The SV Ranch lay quiet in the night, seemingly asleep. It was late, but there was a light burning in the galley. A man emerged, yawning, carrying a rifle in the crook of his left arm. He paused to light a cigaret and watched as another man came up, also armed, from the corral side of the ranch.

"How's it going, Red?"

"Quiet," the other said. He paused by the galley steps, a lean, hard, stoop-shouldered man with thinning reddish hair. "Getting tired of it, Les. Sentry duty." He looked off into the night, contempt in his eyes. "Well, them sheepherders ain't gonna make another try—"

He broke off, swinging around as a rider came down the tree-shadowed road to the ranch. Les brought his rifle around, holding it ready. They couldn't see the rider yet, but they heard him. Les made a motion with his head, and Red slipped off, moving into the shadows by the corral.

The rider came on, making no attempt at stealth. Les waited, away from the weak spill of light through the galley door, barely seen near the galley wall.

He could see the rider now, a vague shape on the road. *If he was one of the sheepmen, he was either a decoy or a damn fool,* Les thought.

The man rode slowly now, his hands up high. He moved into the yard and stopped a dozen feet from the galley. He looked around, not seeing anyone. His voice was a bit strained as he called:

"Hello! Anyone inside?"

Les moved toward him, his rifle leveled. He did not know the man, but he did not look like a sheepherder. Nor was he a Box Circle rider.

"You lost, stranger?"

Reno Smith shook his head slightly. "Not if this is the SV," he said. "I'm looking for the Rio Kid!"

Les stiffened, surprise sending a shock through him. Red came up behind Smith. "Who are you, mister?"

"Smith," the man on horseback said thinly. "Reno Smith."

Red glanced at Les. Les frowned. "Ain't nobody by

that name here, Smith. Reckon you got yoreself mixed up—"

"No," Smith said. He glanced toward the bunkhouse. "I've got to see the Kid."

"Reno Smith, eh?" Les made a motion with his rifle. "All right, mister; step down. We'll wait in the galley." He turned to Red. "Tell Joe he's got a visitor."

Red moved away toward the bunkhouse. Les waited until Smith had dismounted, then nudged him toward the galley.

"Smith—it better be important," he said. "The Kid doesn't take kindly to being wakened in the middle of the night for nothing."

Smith grinned. He sat at the long bench table, drew out a tailor-made cigaret and lighted up.

"Nice set-up," he murmured. "I knew the Kid when he didn't have two bits to his—"

He shrugged at the other's hard look and fell silent. A few moments later Joe Turner came in, followed by Red. The SV foreman had put on his boots and trousers, and he held a Colt in his hand.

He paused as he saw Smith, and a crooked grin showed he was only mildly surprised.

"Still playing the long shot, eh, Smith?"

"Always been a gambler," Smith said. "You know

that, Kid."

Joe put his foot on the bench across the table from Smith and raised his Colt until the muzzle looked down at Reno. "The name's Turner," he said. "Joe Turner. I don't know anybody by the name of Rio Kid."

Smith nodded. "Of course." He ground his cigaret out in the ash tray on the table and stood up. "Guess I made a mistake. The man I knew as the Rio Kid was a friend of mine."

He started toward the door, but stopped as Red blocked him off. He glanced at Turner.

Joe said: "Wait a minute, Smith." He lowered his gun. "How'd you know I was here?"

Smith shrugged. "I didn't. I was on my way through, heading for the gold camps. Stopped off and heard some gossip in town 'bout a Texan who had taken over the SV ranch. Then I saw you come into town once." He smiled. "I stayed out of your way. I didn't know how it was between us, after that Bannister deal—"

"But you figger there's something in it for you now?" Joe's voice was grim.

Smith said: "I'll let you decide that, Kid." He looked at Red, who stood a foot behind him, the muzzle of his rifle close and deadly. "Makes me nervous, Kid. Can't you get him to relax with that thing?"

Joe made a motion, and Red stepped back and lowered his rifle.

"One thing I always remembered about you, Kid," Smith went on. "You liked horses. One special. A big bay. Raised him from a colt, you said, never put a brand on him."

Turner's eyes glittered. "What do you know about that horse?"

"It's here, in the Basin!"

Turner stiffened, his eyes flared with deadly intentness. "You're crazy! That horse is in Texas—"

"He's here!" Smith said quietly. "I just saw that sheepman, Burton, ride him out of town. I know that horse, Kid. I made sure before coming up here to see you!"

"Burton!" Turner shook his head. "How'd Burton get hold of him?"

"Stole him," Smith said. "That's what I heard, anyway. Stole him from another Texas rider—name of Chuck Powers!"

Turner looked through Smith to the man who had twice saved his life. He was seeing Powers again, trying to identify him with the man he had killed. He had not known John Powers very well, and he had never seen his son.

He took a deep breath, forcing the edge of fear from his eyes.

"I thought you'd like to know," Smith murmured.

Turner nodded slowly. Then; "What do you want out of it, Smith?"

Smith shrugged. "Whatever you think it's worth, Kid." He looked toward the door. "You got yourself a nice spread here plus a girl anybody would be proud to marry. Maybe I'm wrong here, but—" he smiled, his eyes wise and cynical— "I'd say that old Mex partner of yours, Durango, is around somewhere, picking up all the Basin beef he can lay hands on."

Red said harshly: "You know a heck of a lot, Smith!" He looked at Turner. "Maybe too much."

"You got yourself a job," Turner said, "if you want it, and a cut of all Durango takes."

Smith shook his head.

"That kind of work never appealed to me. All I need is a stake. Enough, say to buy myself a small saloon somewhere, put in a few gambling tables—"

Joe's smile was bleak. "Five thousand do it?"

"It's a start," Smith said casually. He stood up and walked to the door, brushing past Red. He turned.

"I'll be in town all day tomorrow. But I'd like to catch the next day's stage out, Kid."

Turner nodded.

Smith waved. "Sorry I can't hang around for the wedding." He went out and mounted and rode slowly away from the ranch yard.

Red looked at Turner, fingering the hammer of his rifle. The SV foreman shook his head.

"Too many questions if he was found dead near here." He motioned to Les. "I got a better idea. Get some coffee, while I spell it out."

IX

That same night Chuck Powers camped somewhere in the broken hills south of the SV. He did not light a fire. The night was warm, and there was no discomfort from the weather. A fire, however small, would be a giveaway to anyone looking for him, and he was not sure that pursuit by all or any of the angry men in the sheriff's office had not started.

He was in strange country and in enemy territory. He knew he would have to move cautiously until he got to know his way around.

He checked his saddle bags, but he knew he would not find anything in the saddle Turner had loaned him. He was hungry, but he would have to forget eating tonight. He had been seven months on the trail of his father's killer, and he was used to eating sparingly. His money had run out early, but he had worked at odd jobs along the way, husbanding what he had earned. He had money enough now to buy whatever supplies he needed. But he knew he could not ride into Broken Bow; he would pretty much have to live off the land for a while.

He lay back on his blanket, head pillowed on the saddle, and watched a shooting star dart across the heavens and fade. It seemed like a hundred years since he had left home. He thought of his mother, home alone with his younger sister, Jodie. She had not wanted him to go, but Chuck had been close to his father; it was something he *had* to do.

But he thought of them now with a pang of regret. He had left them to shift for themselves on a ranch that needed more help than they had, and even though he knew the neighbors would lend a hand, he felt he had stayed away too long.

But he couldn't go back now!

His father's killer was there somewhere. He had abandoned his father's black stud in the Basin; this was the first tangible clue Chuck had had in weeks. It was possible, of course, that the killer had gone on out of the Basin. The thought troubled Powers but did not convince him.

He lay there, fitting the pieces of what he had

found into a pattern. A Texan, Joe Turner, had shown up in the Basin and become foreman of the SV. Who was he? Where had he come from?

All the trouble in the Basin started when Turner came. That was what the sheepman, Burton, had said.

It was Burton who had found the black stud horse Powers had been searching for; it was Al Drake who had ridden him to the Box Circle. Neither of these men could be his father's killer.

But Burton might just possibly know who had ridden the horse there and turned him loose. Burton was the man he would have to start with. And besides, he had the bay horse, the Bob horse Powers had ridden all the way from Texas.

Burton would not be friendly. But that was a chance Powers would have to take. He wanted the bay back, and he wanted to have a talk with the sheepman.

He thought about this for a while; then, as sleep began to catch up with him, his thoughts drifted to Sandra Vaughn—the way she had looked when they had gone riding, the merriment in her voice; the look in her eyes. . . .

A sound awakened him. He felt it through the ground he lay on, a low vibration, and as his senses sharpened he recognized the sound as the passage of horses or cows or both.

He lay quiet for a long moment. The stars were still thick and bright above him, but he knew it was late. He sat up and pulled on his boots and reached for his rifle. Whoever was moving out there was coming closer, but he had a feeling that they would bypass him.

He rose quickly as his horse whinnied sleepily and crossed to it, clamping strong fingers on its muzzle. He waited. He could make out the sound of cattle now as occasionally one steer or another lowed sleepily. They were moving along a route that would bring them below him, along the creek that ran its irregular course toward the dark hills beyond.

He heard the jingle of bit irons now, the scuff of leather, the sudden sharp cursing of a man as a branch hooked him.

A voice chuckled softly, carrying to Powers on the still night. "Gotta keep yore eyes open, Cooley. Can't go sleeping in yore saddle."

They passed below him, and now Powers could hear hoofs splashing in the shallow creek flow. He waited until they were gone, then he released his horse and followed, keeping to the high ground above the creek. He could hear them moving up ahead, keeping to the stream. Occasionally a man shouted at a vagrant steer, but for the most part they made little noise.

Moving quickly, Powers reached the top of a small bluff that overlooked the creek. He went down on his hands and knees and crawled to the edge. There was no moon, but the sky was clear, and now he could see the drive—about a half dozen riders flanking about a hundred steers, keeping them bunched up and moving, following the creek bed.

They seemed to know where they were going. They moved the cattle quickly, efficiently, and looking ahead, Powers guessed they were headed for what seemed a black, impenetrable rock mass that lay like a long barrier across that end of the Basin.

A rider detached himself from the moving dark mass of cattle and drovers and rode up the far bank, pausing to look down and ahead of the drive. He was outlined against the stars, a man with a Mexican sombrero and what appeared to be a serape draped across his right shoulder.

Chuck watched them move past the bluff: six men moving a hundred head of cattle, at night! It didn't take that many men to move that many cows, unless they were in a hurry. He would have liked to get closer. He guessed those cattle would be branded SV or Box Circle; they were the major outfits in the Basin.

The sombrero-topped rider, dimly seen, nagged at him. He had seen or heard of this man somewhere. But recognition eluded him. He waited until they faded from sight.

Rustling?

What else could it be? Honest men didn't drive cows at night.

He guessed Al Drake was right. Or maybe his brother had been in with the rustlers and Joe Turner had caught up with him. He thought about this for a while, but he was not particularly concerned with the trouble here. All he wanted was the man who had ridden his father's horse into the Basin and turned him loose there.

He went back to camp and tried to catch some more sleep. But one of the voices he had just heard bothered him. He had heard that voice before, quite recently. The big-hatted rider rode through his thoughts, like a phantom out of the past.

He gave up trying to sleep after a while. The stars were beginning to pale in the sky. He built a small fire, heating water for his coffee, and ate the last of his can of beans.

He saddled then and stood by the SV horse Sandra Vaughn had considerately loaned him. He was thinking that riding to Burton's sheep camp in broad daylight would not be particularly wise, that night would be tactically more desirable. He did not know how many men were with the big sheepman. He knew of one named Cy. But there had been others when he had been trapped and held prisoner in the hills with Al Drake while Burton had gone on to the SV to kill Turner.

He would have to learn the country, he decided—every hill and gully. Burton wanted to kill him, and so did Al Drake. If something went wrong at the sheep camp he would be hunted down and, like a cougar, he would have to know the limits of his territory.

But as of the moment, there were two men who were the key to what he had to know: Al Drake—and Luke Burton.

And in the background, ready to move, was Deputy Lou Borden. . . .

X

Deputy Lou Borden rose early and ate breakfast at the Chinese restaurant. He was a solitary man, a recent arrival in Broken Bow, and not an affable, back-slapping type like Sheriff Orrins. He was in his forties, a man with a private past behind him. He lived in the boarding house down the street, having politely but firmly refused Sheriff Orrins' offer of a room in his house. Lou had told him he was a bad sleeper, often rising before dawn, and he did not want to disturb the sheriff or his wife, Kathy.

He ate his eggs and potatoes while listening to the small talk around him. Few people in town, it seemed, really cared what happened to the big ranchers, except for the merchants who supplied them. They were intent on their own petty problems, or talked with more emotional excitement than knowledge on national politics.

He finished his breakfast and went out, stopping by the law office, and was surprised to find the sheriff in. Orrins looked rumpled, red-eyed and unhappy. He was a small man, not ambitious, and therefore not disturbed by it. But like all men, he had his ego image which at times tormented him. He was cursed with an innate honesty which made him see himself for what he was.

Borden said: "Something wrong, Sheriff?"

Orrins eyed him a bit resentfully. "Couldn't sleep, after last night." He shook his head. "How do you do it? Must be that bachelor life yo're living."

Borden smiled briefly. "Your wife giving you a bad time?"

"No," Orrins replied honestly. "Giving myself a bad time." He slid a bit further down in his chair, feeling sloppily fat in contrast to the deputy's tough leanness. Unconsciously his resentment deepened.

"Guess I'm just naturally a lazy man," he said. "Nothing much happened here for almost twenty years. Came to take it for granted, I reckon. Biggest thing was the war, and even that barely touched us. Lot of excited gatherings, a few fist fights—" He shrugged. "Darn it, Lou—they are my friends! I grew up with Al Drake's father. I knew Henry Vaughn when the SV was nothing more than a log shack and Sandra Vaughn was a baby."

"Things change," Borden said cynically. He was a cold man, seemingly not touched by sentiment the way the sheriff was. He went to the gun cabinet, unlocked it and took down a Winchester repeating rifle. He checked it carefully, broke open a box of shells and slid a dozen cartridges into his coat pocket.

Orrins straightened in his chair. "I'm stuck with you," he said abruptly, his voice hard. "I don't like you, but I'm stuck with you!"

Lou turned and eyed him, and Sheriff Orrins stiffened, his resentment carrying him past caution. "Usually I get to pick my deputies. This time the county commissioners sent you. I had no choice. Why?"

Lou just looked through him, his eyes distant, faintly unfriendly. Orrins felt a chill go through him. He sighed. "Why, you don't even come from around here—"

"I'm from Texas," Lou said. He didn't smile, but there was a glint of humor in his eyes. "Before that I was from Missouri. I've been married. I have a son somewhere; haven't seen him since he was two." He waited a moment, thinking back and not liking what came up. "That's about as much as you need to know,

Sheriff." His voice was hard now, final.

Orrins nodded slowly. "Guess it's because of the rustling that's going on in the Basin, eh? Maybe Al Drake's brother was mixed up in it; maybe he wasn't. And Joe Turner hasn't done a thing the law can hold him for. But, Lou, I don't like him. And as for Burton—" He paused, and Borden put words to what he was thinking.

"Is a sheepman." Lou put it casually. "He doesn't count, does he?"

Orrins flushed. "Reckon I am biased, like most cattlemen, and Burton ain't the easiest man to get along with. He came into the Basin with a chip on his shoulder, but nobody gave him any trouble. Not until lately, anyway."

He shook his head, his eyes going bitter. "I feel like I'm sitting on top of a hot stove with the lid ready to blow. And now this stranger from Texas, Chuck Powers, has blown it for me. I don't know what's going on any more, and I'm too old and too fat to ride around and find out—"

"I'll do the riding," Lou cut in. "That's what I'm being paid for."

He walked to the door, thought of something he should say, and turned. "I may have to knock some heads together, Sheriff." His voice was dispassionate. "Maybe even step on some toes. Some of them might be friends of yours. But maybe it's easier this way— I'm new here—I don't have *any* friends."

He smiled briefly. "Go back to bed, Sheriff," he said. His voice had a kindly note in it. "I'll see you later."

He went outside, and Orrins sat in his chair, staring vacantly at the door. He heard Lou ride off, and still he sat, feeling downcast and ornery and incompetent.

Louella the cat came out from under the stove and rubbed herself against his legs. He kicked out at her, cursing bitterly, and she backed off, surprised, for Orrins was innately a considerate and gentle man and had never treated her like this.

He got up and walked to her and stroked her back. He sighed. "Guess I'll do just that—go back to bed."

At the moment there wasn't anything he felt he could do.

Lou Borden rode at an easy pace along the road to the SV. Occasionally he turned off the road to give his horse a breather. That way he could look back along the road, studying it without giving himself away. Lou had been raised in a hard school where survival depended on constant vigilance, and the grades were life or death.

He saw no one; he had not really expected to see anyone behind him. But one never knew. He was a new man here, a lawman, and if what he suspected was true, he would be fair game.

There were a few hands at the SV when he rode up. They were armed, and they eyed him without warmth, their glances holding him at arm's length.

Joe Turner came walking toward him from the corral. He had been talking to a couple of his men who looked as though they had been up all night. Even from where he stood, Lou could see that the horses in the corral looked hard ridden, tired.

Joe said: "Hello, Deputy." He had a smile on his face, and his greeting seemed genuine enough. He had a curly-haired, boyish openness that was deceiving; he would look young and naively boyish even in his advanced years.

"I'd like a word with you," Lou said.

Joe looked around at his men. He seemed surprised, but agreeable. "Sure," he said. "How about coffee in the galley?"

They went inside, and as Lou settled himself on a bench at the table, Joe checked the coffee pot. There was still enough inside, and it was warm.

The cook came out of the pantry, lugging a sack of potatoes. He was unshaven, in dirty underwear and in a bad mood. He looked angrily at Borden sitting at the table.

"Hey! What in blazes you doing in here?"

Turner said: "All right, Ken! I asked him in here." He walked to the table with two cups and poured coffee. He eyed the cook coldly. "Now go on back to the bunkhouse. That underwear needs a washing bad." He smiled then, trying to soften his words. "Bet you haven't washed it since St. Patrick's Day."

"Ain't had time! Ken Connelly snapped. "Everybody eating at all hours of the day an night—"

"I know, I know," Turner cut in. His tone was affable, but sharpness lay like a knife's blade just below the surface. "Mr. Borden and I want to have a little talk." He smiled again. "That is, if your coffee doesn't kill us."

Connelly took the hint and went outside, grumbling. Joe sat across the table from Borden. He took out his bag of tobacco and deftly rolled himself a smoke.

Borden watched him admiringly. Lou offered him the tobacco, and the deputy shook his head. "Ain't never learned how," he admitted, plucking a small straight black cigar from his pocket. "Usually spill more tobacco than I get between the paper. That's why I stick to these. Costs a little more, but—" he shrugged— "a man has to have some pleasures."

Joe watched the lawman from behind a thin screen of cigaret smoke. "Know you didn't ride all the way up here for a social call, Deputy. Although you're welcome here any time, of course." He smiled. "Hope Powers squared everything with the law."

"How well do you know Powers?"

Joe paused. "Not very well. In fact, I don't know him at all. But he's a Texan; at least that's what he says. And I guess, what with all the hostility in the Basin centering on Texans, I kind of feel we have things in common. And of course he saved my life— twice, in fact."

"You didn't know him before he came here?"

Joe frowned. "Never laid eyes on him." He leaned back and took of a sip from his cup. "I know the kind of talk you've been hearing—'bout me sending for hands from Texas." His tone grew defensive. "I didn't want to, Deputy. Why, I had to offer higher wages to get them up here. But the old SV crew quit on me. All of a sudden I was being bad-mouthed around the Basin. I couldn't hire anybody here. Not much else I could do, was there, Borden?"

Borden shrugged. "Not much," he agreed. He turned toward the door as Sandra Vaughn came in. She appeared upset.

"Hello, Mr. Borden," she greeted him. "I saw you ride up." She looked at Turner. "Something wrong, Joe?"

"Mr. Borden was asking about Powers."

She turned back to Lou, who said slowly: "I'm looking for him. I thought he might have stopped by here."

Joe leaned forward over the table. "This morning?"

Sandra said: "Isn't he still in town?"

Lou came to his feet. "He left sort of angry like, Miss Sandra. Not that there was anything I could hold him for. Took him in for questioning, that's all."

Joe's voice had a peculiar quality; it seemed strained. "You mean Powers is out here somewhere?"

"He might have left the Basin by now," Borden replied. "But I have a hunch he hasn't."

Sandra said: "He told me he was going back to Texas. That was just before you took him back to town."

Borden nodded. "Could have been a ruse, Miss Sandra." He saw the look that came into her eyes, and privately he thought that Sandra Vaughn, at that moment, was a very confused girl. "He did seem quite reasonable and unconcerned, until someone in the sheriff's office mentioned a black stud horse with lop ears!'' He smiled thinly. "That's when he got dangerous.''

He walked to the galley door and paused. "Thanks for the coffee.'' He looked across the yard to where several men had gathered. They looked like tough hands, more proficient with guns than with ranch work.

The deputy looked back at Turner and Sandra. "I don't know who he's looking for, or why. But he's dangerous. I repeat that again, ma'am. If he shows up here, hold him for me, will you?''

Sandra just stared at him.

Turner said quickly: "Of course, Borden.'' He walked to the door and stood beside the lawman. "But I hope he's left the Basin, gone back to Texas.'' His voice sounded sincere. "We've got enough trouble here as it is.''

He watched Borden go to his horse and ride way. After a moment Sandra Vaughn came to stand beside him; he was silent, looking out into the yard, her thoughts jumbled.

Joe said: "A hard man, that deputy. I wouldn't want to be in Powers' boots right now.''

She didn't seem to hear him.

"A black horse with lop ears?" Sandra searched back in her thoughts for something elusive but important. "Didn't —"

"Not our business, Sandra," Joe cut in brusquely. He looked at her searchingly. "Or is it?"

She took a deep breath and shook her head. "No," she said. Her voice was dull, lifeless. "No, it isn't, Joe."

She walked quickly past him and went into the house.

He watched her from the galley doorway, a frown on his forehead. He had made one mistake in the Basin, before he had decided to quit running and settle down here. The black horse he had picked up in Texas—

He would have to move quickly to plug up the holes now. And one of them was Reno Smith!

XI

The limestone and granite cliffs cast their early morning shadows across the rolling grasslands below. For more than ten miles on either side of the creek they made a wall through which no road probed. It effectively sealed off the northern end of the Basin. Beyond those cliffs was a tangle of ravines and brush-choked ridges criss-crossed by game trails. It was a wilderness area that discouraged travel and was visited only by trappers and occasional prospectors.

Its western end was anchored to the shoulder of Squaw Peak; its eastern wall lost itself in a maze of isolated buttes and stretches of desolate badlands.

Chuck Powers eyed the towering cliff wall in the early morning light. He had followed the gravel-bedded, limpid-clear creek to this point, from which he watched it vanish into a gorge that made a steep-walled slit in the barrier.

The cattle and the shadowy riders of last night had come this way, but there was little to indicate their passage: a few steer droppings washed up against a curve in the stream bed; an occasional hoof print in the soft earth of the bank above. . . .

He moved on now, following the stream until it entered the gorge. He picked up no sign of cattle or riders leaving the creek before it went brawling and tumbling through the cliff wall. It was possible, he thought, they had continued on through, although from where he sat it seemed unlikely a hundred steers could be driven into that gorge without risking the loss of most of them.

It was sheer luck that he had been camped just above the creek when they had come by last night. The rustlers, moving swiftly and efficiently, taking advantage of the bad feeling between the SV and the Box Circle and the sheepmen, were stealing cattle almost unmolested in the Basin.

He turned back from the cliffs and rode along the stream bed, passing the point of his camp, several miles beyond he saw where cattle and riders had entered the creek. They had come from the direction of the SV.

He guessed the stolen cattle belonged to the Vaughn ranch.

How many head had Sandra Vaughn already lost? Was Joe Turner aware of what was happening? Or was he in league with the rustlers? It hardly seemed likely. Turner was due to marry Sandra in a few weeks. Why would he steal what would soon be his?

He had an urge to ride in and tell Sandra and Joe Turner what he had seen, but he did not know how Turner would take it. The SV foreman was jealous. He had tried to hide it, but during the last few days he had spent on the ranch his civility had worn thin.

He rode away from the creek now, heading east. Sometime later, just before noon, he hit a stretch of newly erected barbed wire—two shiny strands blocking him off from the range beyond.

He followed it for a mile or so until the sounds of someone digging up ahead warned him. He pulled away from the wire and climbed a low ridge. Riding slowly, he came to a point where he found himself looking down on a linehouse. The wire ran to it, anchoring to one corner of the log structure; men were digging postholes beyond.

A sign in a gate left in the fence, a few yards down from the linehouse, read: "WARNING: BOX CIRCLE

RANCH; KEEP OUT."

A man stood guard by the linehouse, a rifle cradled in his arms; he was watching the men digging the post-holes. Farther on, an armed rider was coming down along the laboring men, heading for the linehouse.

He looked up as he rode, scanning the ridge above the linehouse. He saw Powers outlined against the mid-morning sky and swung sharply away from the men, yelling a warning to them and bringing his rifle muzzle up for a quick shot.

The Box Circle hands scattered. The armed guard by the linehouse swung around and added his fire to that of the mounted man.

A bullet burned a gash alongside the ribs of Powers' horse. The animal plunged wildly, shrilling in pain. The other bullets were high and wide as Powers pulled the hurt animal around and rode down the ridge, heading away from the men below.

He pulled up a mile away and looked back, but there was no sign of pursuit. He dismounted and examined the bullet wound his horse had taken; the animal minced nervously away from his probing fingers.

We were lucky this time, Powers thought grimly.

He mounted and looked back toward the distant ridge marking the beginning of the Box Circle.

Maybe the SV was acting as though rustlers were still no problem in the Basin, he reflected, but Tommy Boyd was thinking differently. The Box Circle was stringing wire now, and his men were riding armed, shooting first and asking hard questions later.

The Basin was a hornets' nest, and Powers knew he was in the middle of it. But he couldn't leave, not until he found out who had ridden his father's horse there.

He couldn't get to Al Drake, not as long as the young Box Circle puncher remained on the ranch. But getting to Luke Burton should be easier.

It took him until mid-afternoon to reach a point where he could look down on Shadow Lake. The high bluffs at the northern end of the lake were beginning to cast their long shadows across the still waters.

Beyond lay sheep country!

He would camp there, Powers decided, until the sun went down. . . .

Reno Smith sat by himself at a table in the Cactus Bar, playing a desultory hand of poker. The saloon had recently opened, and a few townspeople had dropped in for a drink before going about their business; a farmer stopped by on his way back home after buying supplies in town. No one seemed interested in a game of poker, which was usual at that time of day. The real poker players didn't make their appearance until after supper.

This had been Smith's routine since coming to Broken Bow. There was nothing in his long, narrow face to indicate this was not just another day for him.

But as the afternoon wore on, a trace of impatience appeared in his eyes. He had his bag packed, his ticket out of Broken Bow. He was scheduled to leave on the morning stage, and he knew he would go whether the Rio Kid showed up as planned or not.

There was trouble in the Basin, and it would grow. Reno Smith wanted no part of it. But he hated to be crossed, and he didn't trust the Rio Kid.

He got up and went to his room and picked up the letter he had written. He weighed it in his hand for a moment, his thoughts going back to other days when he had ridden with the Kid. After a hard decision he slipped it into his pocket and went outside.

He paused just outside the bar and looked up the street where the road wound into the low rolling hills and disappeared. He saw no one. He walked slowly across the street and went uptown to the telegraph office, which also served as Broken Bow's post office. He dropped the letter into the slot and heard it fall on top of others in the small crate behind the partition.

The old man who sorted and delivered the mail was not in, but it didn't matter. Reno Smith was in no hurry for the letter to be delivered.

He went outside and stood on the walk, smoking a cigaret, and watched Sheriff Orrins come out of his office and go into the bank. Things looked peaceful enough in town, he thought, but he knew it wouldn't last. Not with Durango in the hills and the Rio Kid in the Basin.

He went back to the Cactus Bar and found his table. There were a few customers at the bar now, but none of them seemed inclined to play poker.

He shuffled his deck, cut, slipped an ace out from the bottom of the pack and eyed it with a gambler's foreboding. The ace of spades! An unlucky card. . . .

He heard riders now and, glancing toward the bar window, saw them come crowding up to the rail. He made out the Rio Kid, known here as Joe Turner; the other two he had met last night.

They came inside the saloon and stopped at the bar; Joe Turner ordered whiskey for the three of them.

The Kid seemed in a jovial mood. "Any sheepherders around, Mac?" he asked the bartender. The man shook his head. "Don't want any trouble," Joe continued. "Gonna be married next week. . . . Man has to keep out of trouble."

The bartender agreed with him.

Joe turned and spotted Smith alone at his table. "Looking for a friendly game, stranger?"

Smith nodded. His smile was tight, his eyes wary.

Joe turned to his companions. "I got a couple of bucks to lose. How about you?"

"Five's my limit," Red said, "until pay day."

They walked to Reno's table and sat down. "Feel like a little celebrating," Joe said, smiling broadly. "Last days as a bachelor," he added. "Hear it ain't the same after a feller gets married. No more cards, no more drinking—"

"I wouldn't know," Smith said quietly. "I've never been married."

Joe pulled some bills out of his wallet and placed them on the table in front of him.

Smith said: "The bartender's got chips we can use—"

"No need," Joe cut in. "We won't be here too long—just a little fun, that's all. When I lose this I'm leaving." He motioned to Smith. "Go ahead—deal. Straight poker."

Smith eyed him questioningly. Joe turned to the bar. "Hey, bring us a bottle of whiskey," he called to the bartender. "The best you got. Always play better on a bottle of whiskey," he confided to Smith.

He waited until the bartender turned to his back shelves, then said quickly, in a low voice, to Smith: "Five thousand, right?" Reno nodded, his eyes still narrowed, suspicious. "I'll lose it to you right here. Better this way. It'll make explaining the loss to Miss Vaughn easier."

It was smooth and glib, the explanation, but then, Smith thought coldly, the Rio Kid had always been a smooth talker.

The bartender brought the bottle and glasses. Smith shuffled the cards, Joe cut, and Smith dealt the first hand.

Joe won the first time around. Red won the second time. Both pots were small.

Joe leaned back and said loudly. "Smith, this way it'll take me all day to lose a few bucks. What say we make it a no-limit game?"

His voice carried to the bar, and the three customers turned to give them interested glances. A warning trickled down Reno Smith's spine; he didn't like the look in the Kid's eyes.

"Suit yourself," he said.

Red dropped out after openers; Les followed after the next raise. Both men lounged back in their chairs, watching. Turner pushed all the bills he had into the pot. . . .

"That's it, Smith," he said. "All I got. I'm calling you."

Smith stared at him. There was nothing like five thousand dollars in the pot; a hundred was more like it. He knew now what happening, and he felt the roof of his mouth turn dry.

He made a pretense of studying his cards. "Guess you win, Kid." His voice barely carried to the man across the table.

He tossed his hand face down on the table and started to get up.

Joe's gun came up as Smith's chair scraped back. He fired once across the table and once more as Smith staggered and fell.

"Damn card sharp!" he yelled, leaning across the table and mixing Smith's hand with the discards. "Pulled an ace from the bottom of the deck on me!"

Red went around the table and knelt beside Smith's body as the shocked men at the bar watched. "Got a couple more up his sleeve," Red said, taking two aces he had palmed from Smith and waving them in the air for the men at the bar to see.

Joe stood up and backed away from the table. He

glanced at the bartender, his eyes angry.

"You oughta keep an eye on who you let play cards in here," he accused.

"Never caused any trouble before," the bartender mumbled. He stared at the dead man. "He was leaving in the morning—"

"Yeah?" Turner turned back to look at Smith. "Reckon he planned to make one last killing, then." The grim humor of this was shared only by Red and Les.

He was waiting for the sheriff to show, and Orrins did, puffing badly; he had run all the way from the bank when he had heard the shots.

He came inside and stopped short as he saw Joe and his two men; it took a few moments more for him to spot Smith's body by the table.

He walked slowly to Turner, conscious of the gun still in the man's hand.

"Damn card sharp hooked me and my friends in a poker game," Joe told him. "Just a little friendly game, he said. Then he tried to slicker us. I called him, and he went for his gun."

He glanced at his riders for confirmation.

Red nodded. Les said: "He still had a couple of aces up his sleeve."

Orrins mopped his brow. He looked toward the bar.

The bartender shrugged. "Reckon that's the way it was, Sheriff."

Orrins licked his lips. He felt old and tired and not quite up to this; he wished Lou Borden were back in town.

"Trouble always seems to happen when you come to town, doesn't it, Turner?"

Joe's eyes narrowed. "Not my doing, Sheriff." His tone hardened. "You trying to tell me to stay out of Broken Bow?"

Orrins shook his head.

Slowly Turner slipped his Colt back into its holster. He walked to the table, sorted out money from the pot and slipped what he had taken into his pocket.

"The rest of it is his money, Sheriff. Should be enough there to bury him, whoever he is."

"There'll have to be a hearing," Orrins said. "You'll have to be present—you and your men."

Turner nodded. "We'll be at the ranch."

He walked to the bar and paid for the bottle of whiskey. His voice held a mock sadness. "And all I wanted was a little celebration."

They rode outside and mounted. It was mid-afternoon. Joe looked at his companions. There was one more hole to plug.

He said: "We should make it to that sheep camp by dark."

They rode out of town with the sun on their backs, riding at a steady gait, heading for Shadow Lake.

XII

Luke Burton stood in the shadows of a clump of jackpine on high ground and watched the sun go down behind the bluffs. The purple shadows stole across the lake, darkening the quiet waters. At the eastern end, Shadow Creek began its run across the basin, losing itself eventually in a gorge at the far end of the valley.

Shadow Lake! This was the boundary that separated him and his sheep from the basin—from cattle country!

Luke squatted down, his rifle across his knees. Behind him was his country. His flocks grazed the rocky hills and gullies behind the rock and timber house he had built for his family. He could hear dogs barking in the distance. From the sound he could tell that Cy, his brother-in-law, would be on his way in to supper.

His gaze strayed to the house just below him; there was light in the windows, but no laughter, no gaiety.

All the joy had gone out of living here when his son had been killed. He turned to the small grove by the lake where he had buried young Linsey, and the ache still hurt, sharp and lasting.

A small stone corral, really a holding pen for sheep during shearing time, was off to his left. Inside, a horse paced restlessly—a big bay horse without a brand.

Hate rose up in his voice, choking him. "Come on," he whispered; "come get yore hoss, Texas!"

It was this newcomer, Powers, who had stopped him from killing Joe Turner. He had no doubt Powers, a gunman from Texas, was in with Turner, the man who had killed his son. He knew he could never prove this to the sheriff, but inside he knew. . . .

The shadows stole down past the hard-rock hills, spilling over the bluffs that contained the northwestern end of the lake. He could see the last of the day's brightness on the tops of the hills. In a matter of moments now it would be dark.

Luke shifted carefully, easing cramped leg muscles. He could recall when he had first come to the basin. Old Henry Vaughn of the SV and Tommy Boyd, who ran the Box Circle for an Eastern syndicate, had not minded, although Boyd had made it plain he expected Burton to stay on his side of Shadow Lake. It was poor grazing ground, fading off into the badlands beyond, but sheep could get along.

Luke and his wife had been accepted in Broken Bow. At least, the sheepman reflected, they had not been looked upon with scorn. He had sent for his wife's brother, Cy, as the sheep began to multiply. Finally he had hired other herders: men who knew sheep; men who didn't mind sitting for long, lonely hours in the hills with only dogs for company, a rifle for protection; men whose job was not only to tend the sheep (the dogs did most of that), but also to keep the predatory mountain lions and coyotes away.

It was a job, Luke thought bitterly, a job like any other. But it took a solitary kind of man to stand it. And it was a living. You could eat sheep as well as shear them, and they could get by in country where cows starved.

He looked back at the house. He knew Livia would have supper ready, but he wasn't hungry. He had a sour sort of pain in his stomach these days that never left him. He listened for the dogs again, but they were quiet now.

He and Cy would have to move the flocks farther east tomorrow, he thought.

He stiffened, hearing something down around the

thick shadows by the lake, and eased himself to his feet, feeling a tingling in his legs as blood began to circulate freely again. Warning sent a cold shiver down his back as he heard a shod hoof strike a stone somewhere off in the darkness.

He moved quietly toward the corral. The big bay horse had stopped moving and was listening, ears pricked forward. A whinny, low, friendly and expectant, came from the animal.

Luke halted, gripping his rifle.

Riders were moving at a walk up from the lake. They were bunched together, and for a while Luke could make out only a blob of moving shadow. Then they stopped, and as one rider detached himself and rode toward the corral, he saw there were two others.

The rider stopped, and the others moved up, joining him. The man dismounted, leaving his animal in the care of one of his companions. He came on foot now, walking quietly toward the corral.

The bay pressed up to the stone barrier, head held high. The man stopped a few feet away.

"Glad to see me again, eh, boy?"

Luke stepped away from the trees and called out, his voice harsh: "I've been waiting for you, Texas!"

The man whirled. In that moment Luke had a good

look at him. *Joe Turner!* Surprise held him too long. He had been expecting Powers; he would have shot without warning if he had known it woud be Turner!

He saw the man as he whirled toward him, and he raised the muzzle of his rifle and fired. He had a glimpse of the man jerking, as though he had been hit. Then heavy explosions from Turner's right hip split the quiet night.

Luke staggered back, dropping his rifle. He turned and tried to run toward the house. He stayed on his feet—the Lord only knew how—for more than a dozen yards.

The gun behind him roared again. He pitched forward on his face, tried to crawl toward the light from the window, suddenly went still.

Inside the house, Livia Burton heard the gunfire and stood a long moment transfixed with fear. Then, as silence fell upon the night, she ran outside.

"Luke!"

At first she saw nothing, heard no one. She stopped a dozen steps from the open doorway and looked toward the corral as she heard the gate bars being dropped. She saw a man lead the big bay horse her husband kept there through the gate. She could not make out who it was, but she screamed!

The man turned quickly toward her. But the rifle shot came from one of the riders beyond; it knocked her down. She tried to crawl back to the house. A shot came again from the riders silhouetted against the night sky; she made a plain target in the spill of light from the house.

Livia sighed and went still.

Coming up behind the house, Cy heard the shots. He broke into a run, fear gripping his insides, a cold sweat breaking out over him. He was a gangly, loose-limbed man, barely thirty, homely and looking older than he was. He came around a corner of the house in time to see Turner and his men ride off; Turner was leading the big bay alongside.

He couldn't make out who they were, but Cy instinctively emptied his rifle at them. It was a futile gesture, in the dark and at the distance, and he knew he didn't hit anyone.

He saw Livia first. Farther on he saw Luke's still figure lying face down, and he knew his brother-in-law was dead.

He went to his sister first, knelt beside her, turned her over and saw there was nothing he could do. He began to cry, softly, bitterly. . . .

Stillness wrapped itself around the lonely cabin. In

the distance he could hear Kim, one of his two sheep dogs, coming toward the house. Somehow the animal sensed something was wrong and was coming to see.

Cy barely heard. He was wrapped in his grief, in utter desolation.

Chuck Powers heard the shots from across the lake as he was riding down from the ridge where he had camped. He pulled aside, his senses alerted, his eyes probing the darkness.

A .45-caliber hand gun pounded heavily above the sharp crack of a rifle; then there was a brief interval of quiet; then a rifle opened up just as a woman screamed.

Powers waited, starting toward the sheep camp he could not see. Somewhere, across the lake from him, he heard riders. Then a rifle opened up again, the closeness and rapidity of the shots telling him someone was firing in desperation.

Then stillness clamped down over the lake, and the sound of the riders faded off into the night as they headed back into the basin.

Wary now, not knowing what to expect, Powers rode down from the ridge and found a trail leading around the lake. He followed it, his hand on his gun. He came up from the lake to a small benchland where a clump of trees cast their shadows. Just beyond was a stone corral, but it was empty.

Powers dismounted and tied his horse there. He could see, through the trees and somewhat below him, the light from a house.

It was quiet, too quiet.

He started to walk slowly toward the house and almost stepped on Luke's body. He shied off, crouched briefly to ascertain that Luke was dead. Then, turning, he saw a man kneeling beside the body of a woman, close to the house.

Cy looked up as Powers came toward him. He gave a strangled cry of rage, jerked his rifle muzzle up, forgetting it was empty, and fired.

The hammer fell on a spent cartridge.

Powers, shaken, not wanting to kill the man, knocked the rifle from Cy's hands.

"Easy," he warned grimly. "I don't want to kill you; just to talk to you!"

Cy lunged toward him. Powers slammed a fist into his face, dropping him to his knees. The sheepman looked up, tears of rage in his eyes.

"You killer!"

Powers cut in harshly, "You're crazy! I didn't do it. I heard the shots from across the lake, came to see—"

He heard the dog as it came running around the corner of the house. It came directly for him, leaping silently for his throat.

Chuck dropped his gun and caught the animal before its snapping jaws reached him. The weight of the dog knocked him back. He staggered, still holding the dog, and saw the sheepman crawling for the gun he had dropped.

Powers flung the dog away and jammed his heel on Cy's hand as the man's fingers were closing around the butt. Cy gave a cry of pain. Powers drove his knee into the man's face, knocking him back. He scooped up his gun and fired once, into the ground, as the dog came for him again.

The animal backed off, growling, but afraid now. It knew guns.

Cy groped to his hands and knees, pawing at the blood that came from his split lips.

"Damn you," he said hoarsely. "Why'd you come back? You got yore hoss."

He went after Powers again, before Powers could answer him. He didn't care about the gun in the Texan's hand; he didn't care about dying. Powers sensed the enormous rage in the man; he knew nothing he could say would stop Cy.

He used the side of his Colt now, mercifully knocking the man unconscious.

The dog made another run for Powers, but he fired again, and the dog backed off, fading into the shadows by the house.

Powers waited, listening to the echoes bounce back from the lake bluffs. Luke had other herders; they would be showing up soon.

He bent over the woman; she was past all help. He straightened slowly, his jaw ridging. Someone had ridden there and taken the bay horse; someone had shot Luke and his wife and then headed back into the basin.

There was only one man who would have a reason to do that—his father's killer!

Powers looked down at the unconscious sheepman. Cy thought *he* was the killer. That would be what he would tell Sheriff Orrins—

Powers glanced toward the house. He could smell food on the stove—a supper no one would eat. About to turn away, he saw the dark bulk of a saddle by the door. He went to it, recognizing it at once. His slicker roll lay beside it; his rifle was still snugged in the saddle scabbard.

He went back for the SV horse he had left tied up in the grove and replaced the SV saddle with his own.

He knew how it would look to the law—but then, he knew no one would believe him, anyway. If either Luke or his wife had seen their killer, they were now beyond telling.

He looked back once as he rode away. He knew he would be hunted without mercy—a man who killed a woman was given no quarter here, as in Texas.

But somewhere in the basin was the man he had come a thousand miles to find!

XIII

Sheriff Orrins crossed the street to the Chinese restaurant, the barely risen sun at his back. He cursed Borden, his wife, things in general. He had not slept well since the night Chuck Powers had broken out of his office.

Also, he had not seen his new deputy since yesterday morning. The sheriff had checked in at Lou's boarding house; the man had not returned to Broken Bow. As far as Orrins knew, Lou could be lying dead somewhere out in the hills.

The secrecy surrounding Lou's appointment as his deputy irritated him. He ate breakfast in morose silence. The early morning diners eyed him with some surprise; the sheriff was not in the habit of being visible before mid-morning, unless it was an emergency.

Orrins paid his bill and was on his way back to the

office when the old man who handled the mail accosted him. He had a personal letter for the sheriff among some official mail from Cheyenne. Orrins walked to his office, glancing at the envelope. He did not recognize the handwriting, and Reno Smith had not put his return address on it. The sheriff tossed it aside and ran perfunctorily through the official mail; there was nothing urgent in any of the communications. He dropped them into a small tray on his desk and walked to the door, feeling vaguely irritated and more than a bit uneasy.

There was a dead man in the funeral parlor down the street—a stranger named Reno Smith who had come to Broken Bow two weeks ago; a man who had not bothered anyone, until Joe Turner came to town. He had looked through Smith's personal belongings and found little to indicate who he was. There was an old letter, dated several years back, from someone named Taylor, in Rincon, Texas. Seemed that Smith had done this man Taylor a favor, and he was thanking Smith for it. . . .

Another Texan, Orrins thought discontentedly. Turner had said he didn't know Smith, but Turner could have been lying.

Orrins didn't like Turner. He didn't like the entire new setup at the SV, but he knew there was little he could do about it. Sandra Vaughn was old enough to know her own mind. . . .

He spotted the wagon on the road just outside of town, and Orrins knew immediately it meant trouble. Three riders rode alongside.

The sheriff started to walk up the street as the wagon drove past the first outbuildings.

Cy Walker, lips puffed, eyes red with grief and lack of sleep, drove the spring wagon down Broken Bow's street, his face grim. With him were Luke's three hired hands—older men, uneasy on horseback, not handy with guns. But they rode with rifles across their saddles, their challenge holding the attention of the people they passed.

Orrins came up as Cy swung the wagon to a stop in front of the funeral parlor. Other men began to gather on the walk.

The sheriff said: "What happened, Cy?" But he knew before the sheepman answered.

"Luke," Cy said. His voice was choked with rage. He turned his head toward the two blanketed figures in the wagon. "My sister. . . ."

Orrins stepped to the back of the wagon. Lee Younger, a clerk in the general store, stepped up on the wheel hub and pulled the blankets away from Luke and his wife. A grayness crept over the sheriff's face. He made a motion, and Lee dropped the blanket over the bodies.

"Last night, Sheriff!" Cy's voice shook. "That Texan came for his bay horse. He killed Luke—my sister!"

Orrins sighed heavily. A murmur ran through the group of men on the walk.

"You sure?"

"I saw him!" Cy dragged a saddle out from under the wagon seat and dumped it on the walk. "Luke had his saddle and slicker roll by the house, the bay horse penned in the corral. The horse is gone; he left this saddle in place of his own. I saw him when he came back for it."

Orrins shook his head. "Shooting Luke I can understand, Cy. I'm not saying it's right, but Luke had his horse. But Luke's wife—"

Cy cut in, his voice harsh, "We don't care what you think, Sheriff. I brought the bodies in for you to see. And I tell you flat out we're going after that killer! And we're not going to be stopped by cowmen, ordered to stay on our side of Shadow Lake! We're shooting first, Sheriff!" Tears of rage glistened in Cy's eyes. "You hear me, Sheriff! We're riding the basin, looking for him—"

Orrins felt a quiet anger steady him. Some spark of youth returned, firming his voice.

"You don't have to go it alone, Cy. I'm riding with

you. I want to find the man who'd shoot a woman—"
He turned to the group on the sidewalk. "I want a posse
assembled here in five minutes, ready to ride!"

The crowd broke up, the men running toward the
stables. Orrins turned to Cy. "Get yourself a mount at
county expense. I'm wiring Cheyenne, Laramie, all the
towns in the Territory. If Powers manages to leave the
basin before we can block him off, they'll pick him up!"

He was feeling younger than he had for many years.
Maybe it was the tide of anger in him, the outrage at
what had happened, he thought; maybe it was just that
now he had a focus for his uncertainties.

He strode back to his office, picked up a rifle and
some shells. The letter Reno Smith had mailed to him
lay on his desk, unread, as he hurried out. . . .

Daylight stained the sky behind Luke Burton's sheep
camp. It picked up the rider coming around the lake,
pausing to study the wooden cross marking young Linsey
Burton's grave just beyond. Behind him small waves
fretted against the bank; a bird chirped, greeting the
still morning.

Lou Borden listened for signs of activity, but there
was only a peaceful quiet, a stillness that tightened the
lines around his mouth.

It was possible, he thought, that the sheepman was still asleep, but he doubted it. He knew from experience that ranch work was hard, be it cattle or sheep, and the day's work started at dawn. . . .

He had spent the night at the Box Circle, talking to an angry Tommy Boyd.

"Sure we're stringing wire," Boyd said flatly. "And we're riding line with cocked rifles!" Boyd strode up and down his living room, the good nature stripped from him. "I've been asleep too long, Deputy. I didn't want trouble with the SV, mainly because of Henry Vaughn's daughter. But our trouble started right after Joe Turner moved in. We began losing cows—I didn't know how many until I made a tally count—"

"You think Turner is behind the rustling?"

"I don't know," Boyd shot back. "But I feel now that Al's brother had nothing to do with it. I know what Joe Turner said—"

"The SV has been losing beef, too, I understand." Lou's voice was level.

"That's what Turner claims." Boyd stopped by the big stone fireplace, his eyes troubled. "I want to be fair, Borden. I don't like Turner. But I don't have any proof he's done anything out of line." He came back to join the deputy seated by the window. "My tally shows I've lost more than three hundred head. I'm going to have to explain that to my bosses back East." He shook his head, angry, uncertain. "I know *I've* been losing cows. What I'd like to know is where they've been taken. It ain't easy, Deputy, just to drive that many steers out of the basin."

Borden thought of this now as he looked up the slope to the benchland beyond which lay Burton's cabin. It was too quiet there. . . .

The light strengthened on the lake behind him. He knew that in another minute or so the sun would edge up above the horizon. A jay began to chatter in the trees as he rode slowly toward the small clump of trees on the benchland and looked down at the house.

The door was open, but there was no smoke coming from the chimney. A small ground squirrel ran across the open ground and paused at the threshold, sitting up, listening. Then, with a flick of its tail, it darted inside.

Borden called: "Luke!"

There was a stir of wind in the trees above him. A sheep dog came into view around the back of the house, but it vanished as Lou slowly rode toward the cabin and dismounted.

Lou's eyes were hard. He walked to the door and looked inside. Three plates were set on the table; they had not been used. He went inside. Supper was cold on the wood stove.

He went back outside and studied the ground, knowing something had happened there last night. He saw something up ahead and went to it, kneeling slowly and touching his fingers to blood still damp, turned dark. Most of it had seeped into the earth. . . .

Lou had a trained eye for tracks and small details. He went over the ground, finding where Luke had fallen. He studied the tracks around the stone corral, following them back to where three riders had paused, then one man had gone on ahead. . . .

Three riders had come around the lake from the basin. One of these had killed Luke, he suspected, and taken the horse Luke had kept penned in his corral. *Powers' bay horse?*

But there was another rider who had come from around the lake. He had come later, he guessed, and then had ridden off.

Lou put the pieces together as well as he could. Luke Burton was probably dead. Someone else, maybe his wife, maybe one of his herders, had been shot in front of the house. The sheepman's wagon was gone; Lou could see the tire tracks headed for the road to town.

He could ride after the wagon, he reflected, find out

what had happened. But—he glanced toward the rising sun—the wagon would be almost to Broken Bow by now.

The key to this, he thought grimly, was the lone rider. *Powers?* He was guessing, of course. Powers had come for his bay horse, either before or just after the three other riders. Probably later. If so, he had found Burton dead, his horse gone.

Borden walked back to his horse, pulled out a slim cigar. He had the choice of trying to track the three riders or of following Powers. A smile touched his thin lips. He would let Powers do the tracking for him!

He mounted and rode away from the sheep camp.

XIV

Chuck Powers dismounted and studied the bullet gash on the roan's shoulder, slanting up from the rib cage. It was a shallow wound, but it was bleeding again, and he knew it was going to cause trouble.

He ran his hand along the SV animal's neck, patting him. The roan should be back at the ranch, being treated, but Powers knew he had no choice.

"Sorry, boy," he murmured. "I'll see what I can do for you later, after dark. . . ."

He was on a slight rise of ground overlooking the northern end of the basin, shadowed by an old gnarled oak. He could see the barrier in the distance. A quarter of a mile below him, Shadow Creek twisted and turned, hidden by overhanging trees, as it made its way toward that distant cliff wall.

He had followed the tracks of the three riders out of

Burton's sheep camp, picking them up past the lake at sunup and following them until they hit the creek.

He lost them there for a time; then, moving slowly, patiently, he saw where one rider had left the creek and headed in the direction of the SV. The other two, keeping the bay horse with them, stayed with the creek, going downstream. He had followed them downstream to this point; he knew now where they were headed—through that gorge in the barrier.

One man had ridden back to the SV!

It could be Turner, Powers thought grimly, or it could be any one of the SV hands.

He'd have to wait until dark again, he decided. He had spotted a posse earlier, at least a dozen armed men. He guessed there would be others, waiting on the two roads out of the basin.

He could stay clear of the posse for a while, but sooner or later he'd be run down. He was bottled up here in the basin.

He squatted on his heels, his eyes hard. He was a long way from home, a Texan in Wyoming, a stranger the basin people believed had killed a woman! He knew what that meant in Texas; he didn't figure it meant less here!

He thought of Sandra Vaughn, the way she had

laughed, the way she had looked at him as they went riding. It seemed like a hundred years ago. . . .

He couldn't stay out here forever. he reflected bitterly. He had two choices. He could ride by himself through that river gorge in the barrier and see who and what lay beyond it. Or he could risk riding back to the SV under cover of night, try to see Sandra Vaughn, explain what had happened, and ask her what she knew about a black horse with lop ears and about the man who had ridden him there. He had asked that question a thousand times, but he had never asked her. However, if Joe Turner was the man he was after, she would know. . . .

He was straightening, turning to the rested roan, when he spotted a rider, far off and below him, moving alone. Something about the set of the man's shoulders, the way he sat his saddle, told him it was Lou Borden.

The deputy was following a trail, and Powers guessed it was his. He mounted, gave Borden one last long look, then swung away from the creek, heading into the rougher hills.

He knew he could elude the posse. But could he keep clear of Lou Borden?

He used every trick he knew, and some that came to him as he rode. By mid-afternoon he was back at

Shadow Lake creek, using it to cover his passage. He rode upstream for a quarter of a mile, then doubled back to a point where a shelf of gray rock thrust into the creek bed. He dismounted and led the tired roan up this slant of rock, emerging finally high up on the rocky ridge. He ducked below the rim, finding a pocket among the rocks, shadowed by a tall, almost limbless pine that cradled a hawk's nest a hundred feet above him.

He tied the SV animal there and crawled back to the rim. Lying on his stomach, he studied the land below. He lay there a long time, but Lou Borden did not show up.

He had lost him!

He wanted to believe this, but somehow he didn't feel easy. He glanced up at the sky. It would be a long wait to sundown. . . .

Tommy Boyd strode angrily across the yard and faced Al Drake, standing by the saddled horse, a rebellious look in his eyes.

"What in the devil you think yo're doing?"

"It's my hoss, Mr. Boyd!" Drake's voice was hard. "I found him. I'm riding him!"

Tommy Boyd's neck reddened. He didn't like being crossed by one of his hands.

"I promised the sheriff I'd hold onto the animal." He glanced at the big black stud with the lop ears Al Drake had just finished saddling; it was tied to the corral bars. "Far as I'm concerned, that animal belongs to the law until its owner shows up—"

He brushed past the young cowboy, reaching out to untie the animal, but stopped, his eyes going cold, as Al Drake held the muzzle an inch from the foreman's belt buckle.

"That's exactly what I want, Mr. Boyd! I want his owner to come for him!"

Boyd said roughly: "You fool! Put that gun away! And stay away from this animal."

Al shook his head, his eyes dangerous.

Boyd lost control. "Damn you, yo're fired!"

Al Drake's grin had a reckless tilt. "I jest quit!" He motioned to the horse. "I'm jest taking what belongs to me."

Boyd choked back his anger. "You fool kid—" He shook his head, a man trying to cope with too many sudden problems. "I don't care about the horse. But you ride him out of here, and you'll get yoreself killed!"

He turned, aware of several men watching from the bunkhouse. Suddenly angry again, he waved to them. "Don't you fools have anything better to do?"

They disappeared back inside the bunkhouse.

He turned back to Drake. "You'll get killed!" he repeated. "Dammit, I sort of feel responsible—"

"That's what happened to my brother," Al cut in harshly. "Nobody did anything about it. Some even believed Joe Turner's story about him being in with the rustlers—"

"All right, *all right!*" Boyd made an impatient gesture. "So maybe we were wrong then. But riding out of here on the black horse will mark you for the killer. That is, if he's still in the basin—"

"You know he is!" Al shot back. "And we both know *who* he is!"

Boyd shook his head. "I've said it a dozen times, Al—I don't know, not for sure. And neither do you."

Al shrugged and turned to the horse. He began tightening the holding straps of his blanket roll.

"Wait, dammit!" Boyd said. "That deputy, Borden, was here last night. You saw the way he looked that stud over. Line O brand. A Texas brand, he said. That deputy knows more than he's letting on—"

"I don't give a hang what he knows!" Drake said coldly. "He told me to stay on the ranch. But I jest quit. And I don't have to stay here—"

He paused, looking off toward the road, a sudden

glint in his eyes.

"Looks like you got company, Mr. Boyd!"

The foreman turned hard on his heel. Coming in off the road, a man was riding hard, not sparing his horse.

The Box Circle foreman stepped away from the corral, moving to meet the newcomer. The rider was a townsman, George Reever. He had a rifle thrust in a saddle scabbard, and he was dusty and grim-faced.

"Luke Burton and his wife—shot! Sometime last night!" His voice was strained. "Luke's brother-in-law brought the bodies into town this morning. Cy says it was that Texan did it—Joe Turner's gunslinging friend!"

"Powers?"

"That's him. Sheriff Orrins is out leading a posse. He's got men riding to cut off the road at Cutter's Pass and the stage road at South Fork. He sent me here to see if you could spare some of your men."

Boyd swung around to Al Drake, but the young cowboy had mounted and was already riding.

"Al, he'll kill you!"

Drake galloped past without caring. He was on his own now, no longer taking orders from Boyd. To hell with him and Lou Borden! He had lived long enough with his brother's death on his conscience.

Joe Turner—or Chuck Powers! It had to be one or

the other!

He swung away from the road, heading into the rough country where his brother had met his death. The newly erected barbed wire kept him from crossing over until he reached the linehouse.

The guard at the gate was surprised to see him. Al's gun froze the look on his face.

"Don't ask questions, Nate. Just open the gate!"

Nate glanced down the line to the point where the wire vanished into a ravine. Harvey was riding the wire out there.

"*Open the gate!*"

Nate shrugged and swung it open.

Al Drake rode through without looking back.

XV

Chuck Powers opened his eyes with a start. He had dozed! How long? He had his back against the pine trunk. The shrill cry of the hawk, coming back to its perch above him, had awakened him.

He scrambled to his feet. The roan had moved away from the tree. He found it farther down, nibbling at some grass between the rocks. He brought him back, tied him to the tree.

The sun was low over the western hills.

He crawled back to the rim of the ridge. At first he saw nothing. About to turn back he stopped. Something was moving in the distance; a rider was coming down into the small valley below him.

Borden?

He remembered his father's field glasses in his saddle bag and went back for them.

The rider was following the line of trees rimming the creek. Powers picked him up in the glasses; he adjusted the center focus. The image was clear now— *a rider on a big black horse with lop ears!*

For a long moment Powers watched the man, scarcely breathing, afraid the image would fade away. His hands trembled as he finally lowered the glasses.

He had searched a long time for this man!

He raised the glasses again. The rider was coming toward him. He was nearer now, and disappointment gripped Powers.

It was his father's horse, but not his father's killer. But it was more of a break than he had counted on; he had not expected Al Drake to leave the Box Circle.

He studied the oncoming rider, a hard, cold smile forming on his lips.

"I owe you something, too," he murmured.

He slipped back to the roan, put the glasses away and mounted. He rode down the ridge, away from view of the rider below, crossed the stream and dismounted before climbing the bank. Leading the animal now, he moved cautiously among the trees until he could look up the small valley to the oncoming rider. The man was still too far away for him to see Powers.

The Texan tied the roan to a sapling and unfastened

the rope lashed to his saddle. Drake was headed that way, and he couldn't help spotting the roan. . . .

Al Drake rode slowly, holding his rifle across his saddle. He kept to the river and away from cover; he was making no attempt not to be seen.

He had seen no one since leaving the Box Circle linehouse, but he was not impatient. Sooner or later the man he was after would come to him.

The black he was riding blew noisily, shaking his head. Drake patted the side of his neck. "Long way from home, eh, feller?" His eyes were hard. "Now if you could only talk—"

The black blew again, stopped. A warning whinny fluttered through his lips.

Drake rocked forward in the saddle, alert, his rifle ready. His eyes ranged ahead along the creek bank. He said softly: "See something, feller?"

Then the roan moved up ahead, and he saw it and almost fired. He cursed softly as he dismounted, holding the black's reins. The animal ahead tugged at its picket line, watching them.

Drake shoved his rifle back into its scabbard, drew his hand gun and cocked it. Leading his black horse, he moved toward the roan.

Nothing else moved. He heard the gurgle of the creek below, the drowsy hum of insects in the shade. He was ready for trouble, but it escaped him.

He paused by the roan's side and saw it was an SV branded animal. A recent bullet wound across the ribs and shoulder still oozed a few drops of blood.

He backed off a bit and looked around. Something splashed in the water behind the roan. Drake swung around and stepped quickly into the saddle of the big black, his gun poised. . . .

The rope settled across his shoulders, thrown from behind. It tightened before he realized it was there, pinning his arms. He tried to twist around, but a hard jerk pulled him out of the saddle. He fell heavily, the wind knocked out of him.

Powers came up quickly, a gun in his hand. He kicked Drake's gun out of his grasp, jerked the younger man to his feet and shoved him back against the horse. The animal shied away, and Drake dropped to his knees.

Powers said grimly: "You looking for me?"

Drake's eyes blazed at him.

Powers grinned. "An old Texas trick, waddy." He tugged at the rope, pulling Drake off balance. "Don't want you to get too cocky, figuring you was the only one could use a rope."

Drake loosened the noose from around his shoulders and cast the rope aside. He came slowly to his feet.

"You damn woman-killer!"

Powers' eyes went cold. "I see you heard about Luke and his wife. I didn't kill them. But I ain't gonna argue the point with you."

He looked at the black stud behind Drake. "I'm trading you," he said. "The black for my SV roan." He motioned with his gun. "Ain't had much rest lately. I'll watch while you change saddles." He chuckled, but there was little mirth in it. "It'll take the kinks out of you, cowboy."

Al didn't move. "Figgered that black would bring one of you out," he sneered.

"One of us?"

"You or Joe Turner. One of you killed my brother." His glance dropped to the gun Powers had kicked out of his hand, and he lunged for it.

Powers' quick shot spun the gun away from him.

"Hold it! I don't want to have to kill you!"

Al looked up as Powers came between him and the gun. "Why not?" His voice challenged Powers.

"I could have done that ten minutes ago," Powers snapped. "You were riding like a fool, a plain target for even a cockeyed man with a rifle. If I had been Joe

Turner—aw, forget it," he finished, his voice full of disgust. "Get those saddles changed. Then you can ride that roan back to the SV, or turn her loose on SV range if you'd rather."

Drake's eyes narrowed. "What'd you stop me for?"

"You were riding my father's horse. I thought, at first, you were the man I had trailed all the way from Texas!"

Drake frowned. "Yore father's horse?"

Powers turned and whistled softly. The black stallion lifted his head. Powers said: "Remember me, Mig?"

The black looked at him; a soft flutter of recognition came from his lips. He moved toward Powers, and Powers rubbed his hand across the high-arched neck. "It's been a long time, Mig."

He turned back to Drake.

"This was my father's favorite horse. The man who killed him left his own, a big bay horse, saddle-sore and lamed, in his place, beside my father's body. I rested him until he could run again; then I went after the man who killed my father. I never saw the killer—all I had to go on was my father's horse." He paused. "I had about given up when I heard you say Mig was here—"

Drake said, as if he still couldn't believe it, "You're not a friend of Joe Turner?"

"I stuck my nose into something that was none of my business," Powers said. "I was tired that day, feeling down at the mouth. I saw four men threatening a man who spoke Texas—"

"Close, eh?" Drake sneered. "All you Texans—"

"Maybe!" Powers snapped. His voice was cold again. "I'd do it again, seeing those odds!"

"Even if Turner is the man who killed yore father?"

Powers' eyes flared. "Let's quit playing games, cowboy!" He motioned to the black. "Get those saddles changed!"

He watched while Al, stiff and reluctant, did as he was told. Powers was thinking things out as the younger man worked.

"Three men rode up to Luke's camp last night," he said evenly. "They killed Luke and his wife and took the bay horse I rode here."

Al stood by the SV animal, eying Powers. The curl of his lips showed his disbelief.

"I don't give a hoot if you believe that or not," Powers snapped. "But that's the way it is. One man crossed the creek and headed for the SV. The other two stayed with the creek and went that way." He indicated the barrier in the distance. "They took the bay horse with them.

"I'm going to give you a choice," Powers went on. "I can show you where to find the men who killed your brother. Or you can ride that SV animal out of here and take your chances with Joe Turner."

Al Drake sneered: "How'd I know you won't shoot me in the back?"

"That's a chance you'll just have to take!" Powers snapped. He shoved his gun back into his holster and mounted his father's black. "Make up your mind!" he said coldly.

Drake looked down the valley toward the distant barrier. He looked up at Powers. And he made up his mind. He picked up his Colt, holstered it and swung aboard the roan.

"Show me!" he said. His tone was cocky; he still didn't quite believe Powers. "All I want is a crack at the man who killed my brother!"

XVI

Joe Turner watched Sheriff Orrins and a half-dozen grim-faced men pull up before the ranch house, a flicker of apprehension in his eyes. He had not slept well, the pain from the flesh wound in the upper part of his left arm making him restless. He had a clean shirt on now, hiding the bandage. He put a smile on his face as he crossed from the bunkhouse to join the mounted men.

Sandra Vaughn was on the porch steps, looking down at the saddle Sheriff Orrins had dropped in front of her.

"This your saddle, Sandra?"

Orrins had known this woman almost from the time she was born; it explained the familiarity.

Sandra shook her head. "I don't know. It's just a saddle."

Turner came up and lifted the saddle skirt. A small SV iron had been branded into the leather. He looked up at Orrins.

"It's the saddle Powers used when he rode out of here. We loaned him a roan horse, too."

Sandra's voice was strained. "Anything happen to Chuck?"

One of the men behind Orrins said harshly: "Not to him, Miss Sandra—not yet! He killed Luke Burton last night. And—" his voice shook a little— "Luke's wife!"

Sandra Vaughn staggered a little, as though she had received a physical blow. She held onto the porch railing for support.

"If you know anything, Sandra," Orrins said bluntly, "it'll help. Luke's men are combing the basin. If they run into Powers they'll kill him! I can't stop them. I'm not sure I want to—"

"I don't believe it!" Sandra's face was white. Her gaze ranged over those grim, silent men, went to Joe Turner for support. "Chuck couldn't kill a woman."

"It's hard for me to believe, too, Sheriff," Turner said. "Maybe Powers rode up to see Luke about his horse—that big bay he owned—and they got into an argument. Maybe he had to shoot Luke—"

"His wife, too?"

Joe paused, shaking his head slowly.

"Cy was there," Orrins went on. "He said Powers killed them both. Until I learn different, that's what I have to go on."

He glanced toward the corrals, where several SV hands were watching. "I came to ask you for every rider you can spare. Tommy Boyd is sending some of his hands, too. We're going to comb every hill and ravine in the basin—"

Turner shrugged. "Powers could be out of the basin by now."

"I don't think so. I've got men covering the roads out. I've sent wires to every law office within a hundred miles." Orrins shook his head. "Powers won't get away. I just want to pick him up before Luke's men do."

He looked at Sandra Vaughn. "I'm sorry, Sandra. I felt you should know."

She nodded slowly. "Thank you, Sheriff." She pulled back from the railing; she did not look well. "Mind if I go inside?" Her smile was strained. "I've got a headache."

Joe Turner watched her go into the house, his eyes narrowed, a jealous twinge in his stomach.

He turned back to Orrins. "Don't see yore deputy, Borden. He leading another posse?"

Orrins shook his head, his eyes worried. "Haven't

seen him since yesterday morning.''

Joe frowned. "He stopped by here yesterday; we had coffee. He asked about Powers.'' Turner broke off, dropping his gaze; he gave the impression of a man who had more to say but did not want to.

Orrins said sharply: "You thinking of something, Joe?''

Turner took a moment before replying. "Just hope that yore deputy didn't run into Powers, Sheriff.'' He looked up at Orrins now, his tone troubled. "Look—it ain't right for me to say anything about Powers—he did save my life. But—'' his eyes were steady on the sheriff's face, alert to any giveaway expression— "he asked me about a couple of names while he was here. Kinda casual like, but I knew they meant something to him, like they were close friends of his.''

"Names?''

"Durango,'' Turner said. He watched the sheriff's eyes. "And the Rio Kid.''

The sheriff frowned. "Don't mean anything to me.'' He turned to the men at his back. All of them shook their heads.

Joe smiled, his thoughts at ease now. "Thought you ought to know, Sheriff.''

He called the men by the corral over. "Saddle up;

yo're riding with the sheriff. You'll take orders from
him, but you'll draw yore pay from the SV."

He turned back to the sheriff. "Fair enough?"

Orrins nodded. He waited until the SV hands had
mounted and joined him. Then he rode out of the
Vaughn ranch yard, Sandra Vaughn's stricken face in his
mind, troubling him. He had watched Henry Vaughn's
little girl grow up. Who would have thought her life
would become entangled with two Texans, both strangers
to where she had been born.

*Joe Turner or Chuck Powers! Either way, she stood
to lose. . . .*

Joe waited until the posse was out of sight. He
picked up the saddle Orrins had dropped and walked
into the bunkhouse, dropping it on the floor by the
bunk on which an unshaven man slept.

The man stirred, but did not awaken. Joe shook him.
The man turned and struck out, still half asleep, at his
tormentor. Joe caught his wrist, held him and said
sharply: "Wake up, Cooley!"

Cooley sat up on the bunk and ran his fingers through
matted hair. He eyed Turner, still tired and irritated.

"What you want, Joe?"

"We'll talk after you get some coffee into you. I

don't want you falling asleep on me. . . ."

"Ain't had a good night's rest in a week," Cooley complained. He pulled on his pants, tugged on his boots. He scratched his head again, but he was awake now, scowling.

"What happened?"

"The sheriff was in here a few minutes ago, with a posse."

Cooley's eyes cleared quickly. He reached for his gun belt, strapped it on.

"They're gone," Turner said. "They're out looking for Powers."

"A posse, eh?" Cooley frowned.

"The sheepmen, too," Turner added. "They're scouring the basin. The Box Circle's got men out, too. Cutter's Pass is blocked off; so's the stage road to Laramie."

Cooley looked at him, his lips tight, hard. "Reg'lar hornets' nest, eh?"

"Get word to Durango. Tell him to lay low. I'll ride in to see him as soon as things quiet down in the basin."

Cooley said levelly: "You better see him soon. Durango's getting impatient. It's getting tougher picking up Box Circle cows. Boyd's got men stringing barbed wire and riders running shotgun on it—"

"He's got five hundred SV steers," Joe said harshly.

"Add that to what he's picked up of Box Circle—"

"It ain't enough," Cooley cut in. "He was goin' to tell you himself when you saw him. Durango wants in, Kid—in here!" The raw-boned longrider made a sweeping gesture that took in all of the SV. "Durango wants to go respectable, like you. He's figgerin' on kind of a partnership."

"We'll talk about it," Joe said. His eyes were veiled; he turned away to roll himself a cigaret. "Get out there an' tell him what's happened. I don't want him or any of his men showing in the basin right now."

"I'll tell him," Cooley said. He walked to the door, paused. "I ain't a Durango man, Kid." He said it quietly, waiting for a reaction from Turner. "I just want you to know."

Joe said: "What are you getting at, Cooley?"

"It's getting crowded," Cooley said. "If Durango tries to move in—"

"He won't." Joe moved up to the taller man in the doorway. "We'll wait until the time is right. Then one word to the sheriff and Tommy Boyd, and they'll ride through the barrier."

Cooley nodded admiringly. "They'll clean out Durango—and it'll make you a hero—"

Joe shrugged. "I'm through running, Cooley. So are

you. The country's building up." He looked toward the ranch house. "Good place to settle down."

"You got it figgered," Cooley agreed. "Only one thing bothers me, Kid. That deputy, Lou Borden. I seen him some place—Texas, maybe." He frowned. "Where is he?"

"Dead, I hope. If he isn't, we'll make sure later." Turner waved. "Now get yourself some grub an' coffee. Ride easy. Wait until dark to ride through the barrier."

Cooley nodded.

Then minutes later, Cooley rode out of the SV ranch yard. Turner watched him from the bunkhouse door. He was about to go back inside when he noticed Sandra Vaughn on the porch of the ranch house.

He went to join her.

"Where is he going?" Sandra's voice was quiet.

Turner turned. "Cooley?" He shrugged. " I sent him on an errand." He smiled. "Nothing to concern you."

Sandra said: "Of course not, Joe. You do that very well."

He looked at her, puzzled.

"What is it, Sandra?"

"I haven't concerned myself about anything since you came here, have I?" Sandra said. "You've taken care of everything. Fired my old hands. Hired new ones—"

"That's my job," Joe said; "not something a woman should have to—"

"Where were you yesterday?" Her voice was sharp, cutting him off.

"I told you—in town. Had some business—" His voice sharpened. "What's wrong, Sandra? This thing about Powers upset you?"

She was not to be sidetracked.

"What about last night? Where did you go?"

His face was cold now, hard. "Last night—?"

"I couldn't sleep. I wanted to talk to you; you weren't back. You didn't get back until early this morning."

His voice thinned. "Spying on me already, Sandra. We're not married yet."

"No." she said, and there was thankfulness in her tone. "We're not married, Joe." She pointed. "Your left arm, Joe. Who bandaged it?"

He started. Then, forcing a smile: "You got good eyes, Sandra. I got caught on a branch, tore my shirt—" Then, as her face remained strained, he asked: "What is this, Sandra—why all the questions?"

"A big black horse with lop ears." Her voice was a whisper, barely carrying to Turner. "You rode him here that first day when you asked for a job. I remember seeing it. Then, later, it was gone. . . ."

Joe moved up the stairs; she backed away from him.

"You're wrong," Joe said. His voice was steely. "You never saw me ride that horse!"

Her back was to the door; her eyes searched his face. This was the man she had believed in—the man she had promised to marry.

"Next thing you'll be saying I killed Luke—and his wife."

"Did you?" Her voice caught in her throat. It was too monstrous to believe.

"I'll forget you asked that," Joe said. He went to her to kiss her, and she twisted away from him.

He caught her face between his hands and held her. The charming boyishness was gone from him now, the easy smile. "You'll marry me!" he said coldly, "like we planned. And we'll forget about that black horse—"

He pulled her face to him and kissed her, hard and without passion. Then he shoved her back against the door.

"Go inside and stay there!"

She fumbled at the latch, tears in her eyes.

"I'm sending one of the boys to town," he continued, "to fetch the preacher." She turned a white face to him. "We'll tell him we moved the wedding date up a little and decided to hold the ceremony at the ranch."

"No." She wiped her hand across her mouth. "No."

He dropped his hand to his gun.

"That's the way it'll be, Sandra. Just keep yore mouth shut, an' say yes in the right places." He grinned coldly. "Jest like you been doing."

He opened the door for her and shoved her inside.

The cook was dozing in the galley. Turner awakened him. "Everybody else is gone," he said. "You'll have to do."

"Do what?" the cook mumbled.

"Fetch the preacher from Broken Bow. We're gonna have a wedding here tomorrow."

XVII

Powers watched Al Drake hunker down on his heels in the shadow of a big rock and lick his cigaret into shape. The young cowboy's eyes were wary. He had gone along with Chuck, but he wasn't convinced, and Powers knew he'd have to watch him closely.

"We'll hole up here," Powers said, "until it gets dark. Then we'll ride in—"

"In the dark?" Al's voice was thin, suspicious.

"It was dark when they drove those cows into the gorge," Powers replied coldly. "If they could do it, we can."

"Sure," Drake sneered. "An' for all I know, there's a coupla men waiting just inside. Texas pals of yores. I won't have a chance—"

"You haven't got a chance now!" Powers snapped. "If I was in with them, why haven't I killed you before? What's the percentage in bringing you all the way here?"

Drake settled back, scowling, and chewed on this for a while. His gaze strayed to the two horses they had tied up in the hollow beyond.

"Rustling his own beef?" His tone was skeptical. "Why should Joe Turner do that?"

Powers shrugged. "Maybe he didn't start out that way. Didn't know how the Vaughn girl would take to him at first." But it puzzled Powers, too.

He looked down on the creek below them; over to the barrier, now less than a quarter of a mile away. The shadows were lengthening across the end of the basin. On the slope above them, the last of the sunlight was fading. . . .

Al shifted his weight. "Guess I have to trust you, Texas." There was still an edge of reluctance in his voice. "Haven't trusted anybody since Harry died."

He scraped a match on the rock beside him and lighted up. "Grew up here," he went on idly. "But my folks were from Missouri. They died—both Ma an' Pa— when Harry an' me was kids. Yellow fever." He looked back in time for a moment, his guard down. He was just a boy, barely out of his teens. . . . "I like it here— I guess I'll stay. . . ." His voice sounded lonely, though.

But it sent Powers' thoughts winging back to Texas, to the mother and sister he had left behind. . . .

"You going back to Texas?" Al asked the question twice before Powers heard him.

Chuck looked at him. "Reckon." He got up, stretched. "Never figgered to be away this long."

Powers' black horse lifted his head and looked up the slope, but neither man noticed.

Al said: "You know, Texas—"

"Powers!" Chuck snapped. "Let's stick to it, cowboy!"

Al grinned. "Touchy, eh? Well, as long as yo're being uppity about it, mine's Al Drake. If it's too much to get out all at once, Al will do!"

Powers grinned. "All right. Al—what were you going to say?"

Drake shrugged. "Guess it wasn't important—" He broke off, turning slightly to look upslope.

"Hear anything?"

Powers waited. Down in the hollow, the black stud whinnied softly.

"Up there." Al pointed. He got to his feet, reached for his rifle. "I'll circle around—"

"You'll stay right where you are, both of you!" The voice came from behind them; it was quiet, level and deadly.

Drake stiffened.

Powers didn't move. But his voice was cold, questioning. "Borden?"

The man behind them chuckled. "You got a good ear, Powers." He moved up to join them. "Turn around. Don't make any sudden moves!"

Powers turned. Drake eased away from the rock where he had been squatting, his rifle held down by his side.

Lou Borden came up out of the shadows, limping a little. His pants were torn at the right knee, and dried blood caked his kneecap. He had a rifle in his hands, but the gun thonged down at his right hip was just as deadly.

He said to Powers: "Been trailing you since sunup, all the way from Luke's sheep camp."

Powers eyed the rifle in the lawman's hands.

"Would have gotten to you before, but I fell in the creek and bashed my knee." His voice was hard, but there was a faint twinkle in his eyes.

He looked at Drake. "You ride around like a damn fool. Don't know why you didn't get yore head shot off a long time ago."

Drake said angrily: "You sound jest like Tommy Boyd. Jest because I ain't got gray in my beard an' rheumatism in my joints—" He paused, glaring at Borden. "Who in the devil are you, anyway?"

Borden ignored the question. He looked upslope and

whistled softly.

A hundred yards away, a horse moved into view and began to pick its way down to them.

Powers' eyes held a glint of admiration.

"I didn't want to have to shoot either of you two fools," Borden said casually. He waited until his horse joined them; then he thrust his rifle into the saddle scabbard and slapped it on the rump gently, sending it to join the other two in the hollow.

Powers eyed this strange lawman, his gaze puzzled. "I didn't kill Luke," he said. "And I didn't—"

"I know you didn't," Borden cut him off. He looked at Drake. "Got any more of that tobacco? I ran out of cigars."

Drake held out the sack of Bull Durham and papers, his eyes sullen. He was still smarting at the deputy's remarks.

"Cy said Powers killed them," he mumbled. "There's posses out looking for him—"

"I saw them," Borden said. "Bunch of fools, riding up and down the basin." He turned back to Powers. "Who's got the bay horse you rode up here?"

"One of the killers who shot Luke."

Borden nodded. "Figgered it was the Rio Kid. And where there's the Kid, there's Durango."

Powers stared at him. Al Drake moved restlessly; he

was a brash young man. "What you mumbling about, Deputy? Who's the Rio Kid—and Durango?"

But Powers' mind was slipping back to the sombrero-topped rider he had followed two nights ago. The name clicked now, reminding him of a description from the past—a name feared and wanted in Texas.

Durango!

Borden limped to a rock, sat down and began rolling himself a cigaret; he was not very good at it.

"Been riding all day," he said. "Good to set down for a while. . . ."

Al eyed him in disgust. "The sheriff's out there, riding all over—"

"Do him good," Borden grunted. "He's been getting fat."

Powers said: "Who's the Rio Kid?"

"The man who killed yore father," Borden said. "Goes by the name of Joe Turner here." His voice was casual; he held out a hand to Drake. "Got a match?"

Powers was stiff, staring at him. Drake handed him the match, not knowing what to say.

Borden chuckled. "Saved his life twice, I heard." He looked at Powers above the quick flare of his match. "Guess it comes as a shock, eh?" He ground the match under his heel. "That's what threw me off at first. Had to be sure you weren't just another Texas gunslinger coming up to join the Kid and Durango.''

Al Drake said angrily: ''How do you know all this?''

Borden slipped his wallet from his coat and flipped it open. A silver badge with a lone star enclosed within a circle was pinned to the inside.

''Name's Captain Lou Borden, Texas Ranger. Up here on special assignment—get Durango and the Kid—''

Al Drake wheeled away. ''Another damn Texan!'' He was displeased. ''Ain't there anybody left back there?''

Borden grinned. ''Case yo're interested, either Durango or the Kid killed yore brother. What I haven't figgered out yet is where Durango's hiding.''

Drake came back, pointed to Powers. ''He says he knows.''

Powers said: ''They're somewhere behind that wall, Borden.'' He explained what he had seen. ''That rider with the sombrero must have been Durango.'' He paused, eying the lawman. ''If you know all this, why'd you let them think I—''

''Wanted to let the Kid feel easy,'' Borden said. He got to his feet, testing his knee. ''Let you run around as bait; figgered either the Kid or Durango would make a wrong move. The Kid did, killing Luke and his wife, going after that bay horse of his.''

He looked toward the barrier, now barely seen in the

fading light of day. "Guess it'll have to be us three, going in. If we try to flag Orrins down, it'll take us a day to explain to him. By then Durango will be gone."

Powers said harshly: "I'm going after Turner. I don't care about Durango!"

Borden's eyes went hard. "Turner'll keep. He's got a stake in staying; he won't run. We'll take Durango first." His hand moved, and his gun came up. "That's the way it'll have to be!"

Powers took a deep breath and nodded.

Al Drake said disgustedly: "Damn Texans, always taking over." But there was a grudging admiration in his eyes. "All right, Captain—we'll take Durango first!"

The shadows thickened on the slope. The country was wilder here, rocky and ravined. The three men moved closer to the creek; they could hear the water rushing through the gorge now.

Powers said: "Borden and I are new here, Al, but maybe you know. What's behind those cliffs?"

"Canyons, ravines—bear and deer country." He chewed on a dried stem of grass. "Went in there once with my brother. Packed in. Didn't follow the creek; didn't know about it. Down where the cliffs tail off, over by sheep country, couple of trails lead in."

Borden said: "Guess that's why Durango ran Burton's sheep off a cliff. Was warning him to keep away."

Powers frowned. "Any place where a sizable herd of stolen beef could be kept?"

Drake scratched the stubble on his chin. "Come to think about it, there was a valley—small like, too." He turned to the lawman.

"Grew up here—" he scowled— "an' I never knew there was a way in through that gorge. How come a stranger like Durango found out?"

Borden shrugged. "Owlhoot news. From the Canadian border to the Mexican line, they pass the word along." He ground the butt of his cigaret under his heel. "Well, let's get on with it."

Powers said: "Not just yet, Captain." He had moved back a bit and was facing away from the barrier. His voice dropped to a whisper. "Somebody's coming."

In the silence that followed, the three of them heard it—the pacing of a horse in the stream below.

Borden, Powers and Drake crawled to the lip of the overhang and looked down. It was dark now; they couldn't be seen.

They heard the rider first; then they saw him, a shadowy figure, heading for the gorge ahead.

Powers waited until the man had passed; then he turned to Borden. "An SV rider name of Cooley," he whispered. "Saw him when I was laid up—"

Borden nodded understandingly.

They waited until Cooley had disappeared into the mouth of the narrow canyon, then they crawled back to their horses and mounted. They made their way down to the creek and followed Cooley into the gorge.

Darkness closed around them. Above them the stars shone through the slit in the towering walls. The sound of rushing water grew louder, booming in the gorge. Al's horse slipped, almost lost its footing. Al cursed.

Borden pulled up. There was nothing they could see ahead, but the sound of the water warned them.

He looked at Powers. "Water's getting fast an' deep. They couldn't have driven cows through here."

Powers said: "We'll back-track. They must have left the creek somewhere."

They rode slowly, the horses feeling their way back. Suddenly Powers gripped Borden's arm. The three of them stopped.

A small rock and earth slide was trickling down off to their left. They waited, but the slide seemed to have stopped.

They eased toward the bank they could barely see in the darkness. Powers dismounted. He felt around with his hand, thigh deep in water. He followed a shelf of rock up out of the creek, his fingers exploring the grooves and scar on the stone—grooves made by the passage of iron-shod hoofs.

He stepped back and mounted.

"They went this way," he whispered.

Borden and Drake followed him out of the rushing creek, up the shelving rock. It sloped upward and broadened as they rode. The booming from the creek began to diminish as they climbed. The gorge opened up above them. The starlight was brighter now, lightening the darkness.

Up ahead a rider showed against the stars.

Powers pulled up; Borden and Drake stopped alongside. They waited, watching the shadowy figure top the break in the canyon. . . .

His voice came back to them. "It's me, Charley! Cooley!"

They didn't hear Charley's answer. Cooley rode on and disappeared from their sight.

Powers glanced at Borden. "They've got a guard up there."

Borden nodded. He reached down in his boot and slipped a knife from its sheath.

"Old Indian scout trick," he said. His voice was flat. "Hold my horse. I'll go up ahead."

XVIII

Durango was talking to Red and Les Owens when Cooley rode up. They were in front of the lean-to Durango used as his camp. A fire glowed brightly, sending shadows shimmering across the small lake.

Durango was a big man—broad, powerful, but not tall. Red topped him by at least four inches, but Durango easily looked bigger, standing before the two SV men.

The Mexican had his right foot on a log next to the campfire, close to an axe imbedded in the wood. He was scowling, dissatisfied, his right hand sliding up and down his leg, brushing against the holster tied down on his thigh. Red and Les were leaving, their saddled horses waiting just behind them.

"Tell him—" the Mexican outlaw said harshly—"you tell the Kid I'm through waiting. I want to see him now."

Red nodded nervously. Les eyed the rifle Durango kept propped against the lean-to. Durango was a man of violent moods. . . .

"We'll tell him—" Red began, then turned as Cooley stopped on the other side of the fire.

Cooley dismounted and came toward them.

Red was glad to see him. But there was surprise in his voice as he said: "Didn't expect you up here, Cooley. Something wrong?"

Cooley shrugged. "The Kid wants you back—both of you."

Les said: "We were on our way." He looked at Durango. "We'll tell the Kid what you said."

They mounted. Red looked off across the lake to where most of the stolen cows were bedded. Durango's riders were out there. They were Mexican, a clannish bunch, and they kept to themselves whenever the Kid's men showed up.

It is better that way, Red thought. . . .

He said to Cooley: "What does the Kid want me to do with his bay horse?"

"Leave him here," Cooley said promptly.

Red started to swing away. Les asked: "You staying?"

Cooley shook his head. "Join you in about ten

minutes."

Les grinned. "I'm tired of sleeping on the ground. The bunkhouse and Cookie's chow will look good to me."

Cooley said quickly: "Wait for me at the mouth of the gorge!"

Red looked back. "What is it, Cooley? Trouble?"

Cooley nodded. "There's a half-dozen posses sweeping the basin!"

Red nodded. "Figgered they'd be." Then: "They catch Powers yet?"

Cooley shook his head. He watched as Red and Les swung away from the campfire, heading for the crack in the hills cupping the valley.

Durango had waited in silence, anger gathering behind the scowl on his face.

"I was expecting the Kid," he said now, "not you. Why he send you, huh?"

"Wouldn't look right just now, him leaving the ranch." Cooley was uneasy. "He sent me to tell you to lay low for a while. No more raids on SV cows. Too dangerous—"

Durango took his foot off the log and looked toward the far end of the valley.

"I don't trust him," he said softly. "I'm riding back

with you."

Cooley stiffened. "No," he said quickly, and he knew it was a mistake as the word tumbled from his lips. He saw the Mexican outlaws eyes narrow; the man's bulk loomed up, big and menacing.

"The Kid doesn't want me down there, eh? He wants me here, holed up like a rat. A thousand cows belonging to the basin ranchers—"

Cooley moved back a pace, tensing. Durango grabbed Cooley by the shirt front and shook him. "I know the Kid!" he snarled. "He's got it made down there. He lets me and my men pick up a few cows; he kills the sheepman and his wife; he stirs up trouble. Then, when the time is right, he says to the sheriff, 'Up there, Sheriff—up there behind that wall—there is a Mexican outlaw hiding with all the stolen cows!' " He shook Cooley again, rattling his teeth; his voice grated with suppressed violence. "That is right, huh, Cooley?"

Cooley was not a good actor. Even in the poor light from the flickering fire, the truth of what Durango was saying showed on his face.

"Hah, I am not a fool!" Durango snarled. He shoved Cooley away from him and stepped back to the log. "You wait—I'm gonna ride with you—"

He saw Cooley move then, and he reached for his

gun. The bullet hit him high up in the chest, and he dropped his Colt. He staggered, bent, reached for the axe on the log, and threw it at Cooley in a backhand, desperate motion.

The blade caught Cooley in the face, slicing through his jaw. Cooley dropped to his knees, pawing at his face, blood spurting through his fingers.

Durango staggered to his rifle. He picked it up, levered a shell into place and walked back to Cooley. The man was drowning in his own blood and didn't see him. Durango fired twice. . . .

He turned slowly as four men came running up. They were his riders, not the Kid's—Mexicans out of Sonora. They took *his* orders.

He walked to the log, sank down on it and ripped his shirt away from Cooley's bullet wound. It was high up, under his right collarbone.

"Tomas," he said heavily, "get the bullet out!"

The young Mexican looked at his companions. "I am not a doctor, Durango—"

"The bullet!" Durango grated. "It must come out! Get your knife—"

He shifted slightly, turning to an older man beside Tomas. "There is a bottle of tequila inside," he said. "Get it, Mareno."

He lay back, his chest bared; the blood oozed steadily from the hole in his chest.

Tomas stood by, the knife in his hand.

"Don't be afraid," Durango said. He managed a smile. "You get the bullet out. Then I rest. In the morning, we ride."

He turned to look at Cooley's body; he spat on the ground. "The Kid wants us bottled up here. But we will fool him, eh?"

Mareno came out with the bottle of tequila. He paused, looking off toward the break in the valley.

"You hear that?"

Tomas looked at him; the others shook their heads.

"Hear what, Mareno?" Durango turned his head to look.

"Someone shooting."

Tomas said: "I heard nothing."

Durango lay back. "Hurry," he said. He took the bottle from Mareno's hand, uncorked it and titled it to his lips.

"Begin!" he instructed Tomas. "Do not be afraid."

Chuck Powers and the young Box Circle cowboy waited in the darkness of the gorge, looking up to the point where first Cooley and now Lou Borden had disappeared. It was damp where they were, gloomy. Below them, the river made a steady, rushing sound.

They waited for what seemed hours. Finally something moved up ahead—a shadow coming toward them.

Powers drew his gun, motioning Drake away from him.

"Lou?" His voice was meant to carry just far enough.

"Easy," Lou's voice came back. "It's me. Charley's quiet. We can go now."

Powers relaxed. Drake edged his horse up again; he was holding the reins of Borden's animal.

The Ranger came up, limping badly. He swore with light humor. "Damn these slippery rocks—banged my other knee now."

Powers grinned despite himself. "Keep that up," he said, "and you'll end up a cripple."

Borden swung up into his saddle. "Wanted to look around up there, but figgered I wouldn't have time. Trail dips down into a valley. Thought I saw a campfire way across the lake, but I wasn't sure."

They rode slowly up toward the rim. Drake edged on ahead. He had been following behind long enough; he wanted a glimpse of the camp where his brother's killer was. . . .

Borden's voice warned: "Hold it up, kid. There just

might be—"

Red and Les showed up on the rim, dark figures against the night sky.

Red said loudly: "Charley, it's Red and Les. We're going down—"

Al Drake fired more out of surprise than intent. Red tilted and fell out of the saddle. Les' quick return shot hit Drake. His horse reared, frightened, and Drake fell.

Behind him Borden and Powers fired together. Les, trying to turn back, was killed before he got started.

Al groaned.

Borden rode on ahead, his rifle ready, as Powers dismounted and bent over the hurt cowboy.

"Leg!" Drake gritted. His fingers pressed his left thigh. "Up here."

Powers said: "Can you ride?"

"Just get me up in the saddle," Drake gritted.

Powers practically lifted him. Drake settled in his saddle, his wounded leg dangling free of its stirrup. They rode up to join Borden, who was waiting on the rim.

Borden pointed to Red's body. "Lucky shot," he told Drake. "Bet you couldn't do that again in a hundred tries." He looked off across the valley.

"Durango's camp. Don't know how many are still there with him. And they might have heard the shots."

Powers shrugged. "There's three of us. Let's go see what the odds are!"

Durango lay back, weak, exhausted, half drunk. The tequila was getting to him, dulling the pain.

Tomas was sweating. He paused with his knife blade shining bloody in the firelight.

"Durango," he began, "I cannot—"

"Dig!" the rustler boss grated. "Get that bullet out!"

Tomas closed his eyes and pressed deep with the knife. He felt something hard at the knife point and heard Durango groan, his body go limp.

Tomas looked up at his companions, frightened. "Is he dead?"

Mareno said: "Here, I'll finish it!" He was a stolid man, a bit older than Tomas. He pushed Tomas aside, took the knife from him and dug with brutal callousness, working the bullet out from under Durango's collarbone. He picked it up, holding the flattened lead pellet between his fingers.

"Nice job," a voice said.

Mareno dropped the bullet, whirled and reached for his holster gun. Tomas lunged for Durango's rifle. The other two froze.

The shot from beyond the fire spun Mareno around.

Tomas dropped the rifle, raised his hands above his head. The other two followed his example.

Lou Borden and Powers moved into the firelight, guns in their hands. Behind them, mounted, rode Al Drake, a rifle held ready across his saddle.

Borden eyed Tomas. "This all of you?"

Tomas nodded.

Mareno got as far as his hands and knees, then fell back. Borden walked to him and turned him over. "He'll live." he said to Tomas. "Put a bandage on him."

He turned to Durango, then looked up at Powers coming up on the other side. "Passed out; a bullet in his chest."

Powers pointed to Cooley's body just beyond. "Must have had a falling out."

Borden shrugged.

He turned to Tomas, showed him and his companions his badge. "You are under arrest," he said evenly. "You will stand trial later."

Tomas and his companions said nothing.

Borden pointed to Mareno and Durango. "Take care of them. I want them ready to ride by morning."

Powers said evenly: "I'm not waiting for morning, Lou. You've got Durango. I want the Rio Kid."

Lou nodded. "Ride easy," he said. Then, as Powers

mounted: "Good luck, Powers."

Al Drake watched Powers ride off. Then he dismounted and hobbled over to Borden.

"I still don't know who killed my brother." He looked back toward Powers. "Maybe I should be riding with him."

"Not with that leg," Borden grunted. He pointed to Durango. "He'll talk when he comes to."

He hunkered down beside the Mexican outlaw as Durango stirred. He said softly: "Durango—"

The outlaw's eyes fluttered open.

Borden said: "Remember me, Durango? Captain Lou Borden?"

Durango's gaze held on Borden's firelighted face for a long moment. Then he cursed softly in Mexican and closed his eyes. . . .

XIX

The minister from Broken Bow was uneasy. He had brought his wife, Sarah, along, but she was no help.

They were in the Vaughn living room, the early morning sunlight making a pattern on the floor by the window. There was only the SV cook as witness. Sandra Vaughn, wearing a housedress, looked pale and silent. Joe Turner wore a gun.

It was hardly the setting Reverend Winters had expected. He looked disapprovingly at the bride and groom.

"This is quite irregular," he said. He looked at his wife. "We expected a happier affair, more people—"

"Last minute decision," Turner said. "A private little ceremony—no fuss, no bother." He looked at the girl by his side. "That right, Sandra?"

She didn't say anything.

The minister looked around. There was a piano in a corner of the room. Sandra's mother had played it; it had not been used since her death.

"A wedding without music is—is just not—" He paused, words failing the slight-framed minister. But his wife took the hint. She unpinned her hat, placed it on the table and went to the piano. She hit a few keys. The piano was badly out of tune, but it would have to do.

Sarah Winters turned a smiling face toward the bride and groom. She began to play a wedding march.

The minister opened his book. Sandra Vaughn stood still, lost in thoughts far away. Joe Turner's smile was cold.

He had a ring; he slipped it on Sandra's finger at the proper moment. It was like holding a lump of clay.

The minister finished the ceremony. Joe kissed his wife on unresponsive lips. The minister's wife came up to congratulate Sandra and Joe.

Joe motioned to the small table where he had set out a bottle of whiskey and glasses.

The minister refused; so did his wife. The cook made up for both of them; he killed half the bottle before Joe took it away from him.

He pressed twenty dollars into the minister's hand and said goodbye. He stood in the doorway and watched them climb into the buggy and drive away.

He looked off toward the distant hills. Cooley should be coming back soon. . . .

Sandra was still standing where he had left her. He said to the cook: "See what you can rustle up for a wedding breakfast, Ken. Don't spare yourself."

He waited until the cook had left; then he walked to the woman who had just become his wife.

"You're taking it hard," he said. His voice was cold. "But you'll get used to me."

She turned and started to leave. He watched her for a moment; then, suddenly angry, he strode toward her, cutting her off.

"You were in love with me," he said, "until Powers showed up. What happened, Sandra? What changed you?"

She looked at him, her eyes dead. She didn't answer him. She started to walk past him to her room.

He gripped her arm, swung her around.

"You're my wife!" he said harshly. "You can't change that now!"

He pulled her to him. She didn't fight him; she knew it was useless. He kissed her again, but it was like kissing a block of wood.

He shoved her away from him.

"To hell with you," he said. "I got what I wanted. I own the SV now. You'll keep your mouth shut, like a good little wife, and I'll leave you alone. I can always find my little pleasures in town—"

He heard a rider come into the yard, shod hoofs intruding on them.

Cooley! he thought, and went to the door to see.

Powers dismounted. He had ridden most of the night and he was tired. He stood by his horse, facing the ranch house door as it opened and Joe Turner, alias the Rio Kid, stepped out.

He wasn't expecting me, Powers thought; that was plain to see by Turner's stunned expression.

He put his left hand on the big black's neck. "My father's horse, Kid. Remember? You rode him here from Texas."

He was watching Turner's face, and he went for his gun as Turner drew. The Kid was fast. The shots sounded as one. Powers staggered; the black horse reared, broke away. . . .

Turner took a step forward and fell, face down, on the ranch house stairs.

Powers looked at the blood beginning to slip down his arm from the wound in his shoulder. "Lord!" he murmured, "not again."

He saw Sandra appear in the doorway, look down at Turner's body, then out to him. He started to walk to her, and took a half-dozen steps before he fell. . . .

It took longer this time for Powers' shoulder to heal. He lay in bed at the SV ranch house. Joe Turner's widow, Sandra, took care of him.

Borden visited him before he left for Texas with Durango and the other men he had picked up in Durango's camp.

"I'll tell yore mother and sister you'll be coming back soon?"

Powers looked up at Sandra, who smiled.

"Right after I get married," he told the Ranger captain. "Explain it to her gently, Lou. My mother's an old-fashioned woman; she'll want to know why it is I'm marrying a widow."

Al Drake came along later. He was still limping a little.

"You gonna run the SV?" He put the question bluntly to Powers.

Powers looked at Sandra; she nodded.

"Never thought I'd ask a Texan for a job," Drake growled. "But if you need a good hand, Powers, I'll sign up any time!"

Sheriff Orrins was the last to arrive. He was tired, shame-faced. He tossed Reno Smith's letter on the bed for Powers to read.

"It's all there, about the Rio Kid and Durango. If I had opened it before Luke's brother-in-law showed up with the bodies—"

He looked at Sandra. "I never liked Joe Turner." He turned back to Powers. "I don't know much about you, either. But I hope you'll be happy—both of you."

Powers reached up and pulled Sandra to him as the sheriff went out.

"I'll make you happy," he said to her. It was a promise.